THE AMELIA SIX

AN AMELIA EARHART MYSTERY

Also by Kristin L. Gray

Vilonia Beebe Takes Charge

-THE-

AMELIA SIX

An Amelia Earhart Mystery

KRISTIN L. GRAY

A Paula Wiseman Book

Simon & Schuster Books for Young Readers

New York   London   Toronto   Sydney   New Delhi

SIMON & SCHUSTER BOOKS FOR YOUNG READERS

An imprint of Simon & Schuster Children's Publishing Division

1230 Avenue of the Americas, New York, New York 10020

SIMON & SCHUSTER BOOKS FOR YOUNG READERS is a trademark of Simon & Schuster, Inc.

For information about special discounts for bulk purchases, please contact Simon & Schuster Special Sales at 1-866-506-1949 or business@simonandschuster.com.

The Simon & Schuster Speakers Bureau can bring authors to your live event. For more information or to book an event, contact the Simon & Schuster Speakers Bureau at 1-866-248-3049 or visit our website at www.simonspeakers.com.

Book design by Lizzy Bromley

The text for this book was set in Adobe Caslon Pro.

The illustrations for this book were rendered digitally.

Manufactured in the United States of America

0520 BVG

First Edition

2 4 6 8 10 9 7 5 3 1

Library of Congress Cataloging-in-Publication Data

Names: Gray, Kristin L, author.

Title: The Amelia Six / Kristin L Gray.

Description: First edition. | New York : Simon & Schuster Books for Young Readers, [2020] | "A Paula Wiseman Book." | Includes bibliographical references. | Audience: Ages 8–12. | Audience: Grades 4–6. | Summary: Eleven-year-old Millie and five other girls, snowed in at the Amelia Earhart Birthplace Museum in Atchison, Kansas, are on a scavenger hunt when the lights go out and Amelia's aviator goggles go missing.

Identifiers: LCCN 2019028114 (print) | LCCN 2019028115 (eBook) | ISBN 9781534418851 (hardcover) | ISBN 9781534418875 (eBook)

Subjects: CYAC: Lost and found possessions—Fiction. | Treasure hunt (Game)—Fiction. | Museums—Fiction. | Earhart, Amelia, 1897–1937—Fiction. | Mystery and detective stories.

Classification: LCC PZ7.1.G734 Ame 2010 (print) | LCC PZ7.1.G734 (eBook) | DDC [Fic]—dc23

LC record available at https://lccn.loc.gov/2019028114

LC eBook record available at https://lccn.loc.gov/2019028115

For Caryn and Sylvie.
This book would be lost without you.

THE AMELIA SIX

AN AMELIA EARHART MYSTERY

Dear Amelia "Millie" Ashford,

Congratulations!

We asked middle-school teachers across
the nation to nominate a female student who
most exemplified the eager spirit of a scientist,
engineer, or inventor. Hundreds of entries poured
in. My team and I narrowed the list of remarkable
individuals to six.

It wasn't an easy task.

We looked for students who asked hard
questions, who were endlessly curious, and who
brought a creative flair to math, engineering,
and science. We are happy to say that your name,
Amelia, rose to the top.

You, and five other winners, are invited to spend
the night at the one and only Amelia Earhart
Birthplace Museum, located in Atchison, Kansas.
You'll experience a private tour, sleep in Amelia's
family's quarters, enjoy a scavenger hunt, and see

all sorts of Amelia memorabilia up close—not to mention win prizes from our pioneering partners, Girls in Science and NASA.

We eagerly await your response. If you accept, more detailed information will follow. Should you decline, a wait list of other names is ready to claim your spot. So please, don't delay.

We hope to see you at the Amelia House. And remember, *"Adventure is worthwhile in itself."*—Amelia Earhart

Sincerely,

Nina Hegg

Nina Hegg
President of the Ninety-Nines, Inc., International Organization of Women Pilots

From "Courage"

by Amelia Earhart ©1928

Courage is the price that Life exacts for granting peace.

The soul that knows it not, knows no release

From little things:

Knows not the livid loneliness of fear,

Nor mountain heights where bitter joy can hear

The sound of wings.

CHAPTER ONE

Imagine the worst smell you can think of, multiply it by rotten fish, and I promise you a turkey truck stinks worse. I'd know because I was riding in the front seat of one, sandwiched between Kate, the cheerful driver, and Danni the Body.

At least it was winter. That had to curb the stench.

And by stench, I meant the turkeys' foul odor, not the Body's. That's the thing about Danni—he didn't stink.

If anything, he smelled like the faintest hint of vanilla. That's because he's 100 percent polyethylene. Plastic. But more about him in a bit.

Because, *hallelujah*, we were rolling. Unlike Dad's Chevy, which had fishtailed off the highway twenty miles back. Thank heavens Kate from New Horizons Poultry had spotted us. Otherwise Dad (who was pressed against the passenger window), Danni, and I would be Popsicles in no time flat. Winter Storm Bea had flown in completely unannounced—like Mom used to do—and caught western Missouri off guard, exhausting the area's tow trucks.

"How much farther?" Dad asked. Dad was what Mom called a "chronic worrier." Back when they still spoke.

"Oh, not long," Kate answered, her voice chipper and her brown eyes shining beneath her Kansas City Royals cap. "Say, eight to ten miles. Hopefully, you can spot the Missouri River through the snow."

"Hopefully." Dad pulled his beanie down around his ears and frowned. "Thanks again for picking us up."

Dad was bummed about his car. He'd had it for, well, forever. Since before I was born, and I'm eleven years, three months, two days, and—I checked my watch—twelve hours old. Now Dad's Chevy perfectly embodied Sir Isaac Newton's first law of motion: An object at rest stays at rest. There would be no moving his car out of that ditch until this weather passed.

Dad was stranded and stressed. The opposite of Kate from New Horizons.

"Happy to help," Kate said, smiling. "Every day is an adventure. I like that."

"Not me." Dad blew into his hands to warm them up. "I don't like surprises."

"Yet you travel with a manikin." Kate's eyes sparkled, and my cheeks grew hot, despite the cold temps.

"You got me there," Dad said with a sheepish smile. "I'm a CPR instructor, and Danni's my training dummy."

"Oh," Kate said, putting it all together. "So, do you take Danni everywhere?"

"You wouldn't believe," I said, thinking back to one of my Rubik's Cube competitions when the police showed up and smashed our car window to rescue the "unresponsive individual" buckled inside.

As owner of Lifeline CPR, Dad's entire career revolved around training others to effectively and efficiently respond to a crisis. Or, better yet, to prevent crises from happening in the first place. This was why Danni the Body traveled with us everywhere, though he usually rode in the trunk of the car now, not up front. He'd also cost six hundred bucks, which Dad fretted about for a good three months. No way would Dad leave Danni stranded on the side of the road for someone to steal.

Shoot—thanks to Danni, our neighbor's cat Cleo was on her tenth life. Cleo survived what we call the "Dryer Incident." She was trapped inside for "only" twelve seconds, but the whole ordeal singed the hair off her tail and stopped her heart cold. But Mr. Wilkins got her blood circulating again using the improvised chest compressions he learned in Dad's class. So, as weird as it was that my dad traveled with a manikin, Danni the Body's all right.

Dad's okay too. When he's not worrying over my every move.

"So, tell me about starting your own business. I've always dreamed of having my own floral shop." Kate sighed. "Seems impossible at times."

I smiled. Even though I'd known Kate for only fifteen minutes, I liked her. And not just because she saved my tush. Kate would make a *perfect* florist. She'd probably give each flower a pep talk as she placed it in its vase.

While she and Dad talked shop, I reached into the duffel bag at my feet and found my Rubik's Cube. I wouldn't think about how late we'd be, or how weird it would look to show up in a turkey truck. I was going to take this in stride, like Mom would have. If she were here, which she wasn't.

Her good luck pin poked me through my shirt, reminding me she was probably someplace warm and sunny, like Bermuda. If only *she'd* opened a floral shop instead.

I did a quick checkerboard solve, and Kate clicked her tongue in amazement.

"You can actually solve one of those?"

I nodded, bracing myself for what I knew would come next.

"The only way I could solve that puzzle when I was your age was to remove all of the stickers first." Kate chuckled. Her laugh sounded like wind chimes. The perfect laugh for a florist.

I laughed along to be polite, even though everyone over the age of thirty said the same thing about the stickers. They didn't grow up with YouTube and Google like I did, so they didn't have access to the hundreds of online tutorials on how to solve the original three-by-three. Still, it took hours of practice to get good. And I was pretty sure my cubing expertise had helped me win this overnight spot at the Earhart house. Not many girls cube. Even fewer compete. That's why my first-place finish on the classic three-by-three at Regionals made quite the splash.

"Isn't she something?" Kate asked, and motioned out the window. "The famous Amelia Earhart Memorial Bridge and the Mighty Mo."

"Whoa." I looked up from my cube. Steel beams stretched in an arch across the muddy Missouri River. Bluffs bordered the water, which divided Kansas to the west and Missouri to the east. My skin prickled with excitement. "So, the other side is Atchison?" I asked.

Atchison, Kansas, was where the real Amelia grew up. Amelia Earhart. The first woman to fly solo across the Atlantic Ocean and who, years later, mysteriously disappeared with her plane while attempting an around-the-world flight.

"Sure is, kid." Kate waited for a car to turn in front of us. "Good news. The bridge is prepped and open."

Dad grunted, and Kate gripped the steering wheel as her rig inched across the bridge.

"Welcome to Kansas! You guys haven't told me where to drop you," said Kate.

"The Earhart house, please," said Dad. "Millie has a special invitation."

Kate smiled. "Oh! You're one of the lucky ones. It's been all over the radio today."

"The contest was on the radio?" I looked at Dad, amazed.

Kate laughed. "No, the news about the flight goggles. That is why you're going, right?"

I must have looked confused, because Kate babbled on: "Docents from the Smithsonian Air and Space Museum are here to collect Amelia's goggles for a permanent exhibit, and a big shot at Purdue University believes *they* should be the ones to house the goggles—which are valued at one hundred twenty thousand dollars, by the way. Can you imagine? Anyway, this is the last weekend the goggles will be on display here in Atchison. And no one knows where they're headed next."

"Wow. Really?" My eyes grew wide, and my fingers stilled.

"Really." Kate laughed again. Definitely wind chimes. "Get excited, Millie. You're about to see a piece of history before it's—poof—gone."

I glanced at Dad to see if he'd heard this exchange, and I noticed the worry lines across his forehead had vanished like Amelia's plane. He was listening, really listening, to Kate talk.

The truck rumbled over some railroad tracks. I lifted my

feet to ward off additional bad luck. I mean, sliding off the road was pretty horrible, but then we met Kate, which turned out good. Maybe if I thought of today's events like a math problem, they'd cancel each other out.

We took a right, and then another. Kate shifted gears as her truck climbed a narrow tree-lined street. I struggled to read the road sign through the blowing snow. Santa Fe Street. I clutched my cube tighter. We had one more street to go.

Kate cleared her throat. "I'm not sure I'll be able to make the next turn. So, I may need to let you out—"

"There!" I gasped. A majestic, two-story white home loomed ahead on a corner lot, blanketed in fat, falling flakes.

Kate whistled. "She's pretty as a postcard."

The truck lurched, and Kate steered its massive frame up the hill, as far as the stop sign. Low-lying branches scratched the top of the cab, and an angry cardinal chirped.

I leaned across Danni the Body for a better look. The home's windows arched like those on a church. The front porch boasted eight columns, four rocking chairs—all painted white—and an American flag, which popped against the ivory house and snow. Snow-topped statues of greyhounds flanked the shoveled front walk. The whole scene looked more magical than menacing, like someone had given a snow globe a good, hard shake.

Dad reached over Danni and squeezed my knee. I knew we were thinking the same thing.

Mom would be so proud to know that I was here, at her idol's house. I wished I could send her a postcard to let her know. Maybe then she'd come flying back. To me. To us. Of course, I'd have to know her newest mailing address to make that happen. So instead, I clutched my Rubik's Cube and whispered so low only Danni could hear:

"Mom, it's me, Millie. You'll never believe this, but I'm at Amelia Earhart's house."

CHAPTER TWO

Correction. I was crammed inside a turkey truck—a truck hauling hundreds of live, gobbling turkeys—parked in front of Amelia Earhart's birthplace.

Kate applied the brakes, which squealed like a high-pitched Ferris wheel. A gaggle of girls dressed in bright winter caps and mittens turned their heads and stared from the front porch.

At the truck first. Then at the turkeys. Then, finally, at me.

One girl, dressed in a heavy overcoat, covered her mouth with a hot pink glove. She said something to the girl next to her. They laughed.

I sank deep into the seat and hid behind Danni the Body.

Way to go, Mills. Your weekend is over before it even began.

Dad looked at me and frowned. "Where did your confidence go? Fears are paper tigers."

Blast it. I should have known he'd use Amelia's famous quote against me.

Kate rested her arms on the steering wheel. "I know it's none of my business, but it's been my experience that those girls all feel every bit as jittery and nervous as you. My truck may not be some shiny, presidential-looking SUV, but I guarantee you no one else in the history of the Earhart home has arrived quite like—"

A loud rumble cut off Kate's words.

I sat up and peered out the window. The other girls had turned to look too. Thank God.

"Millie, you've been upstaged," Dad said with a laugh.

I squinted through the snow. "A motorcycle? In this weather?"

Kate laughed too. "Not just a motorcycle. A bike with a *sidecar*."

I watched, mesmerized, as the bike sputtered to a stop. The motorcycle was glossy red, like an apple. Bright orange flames blazed across its sidecar. I'd never seen anything so showy or awesome. The biker killed the engine and lifted the shield on her helmet.

The passenger, a girl, undid the strap beneath her own chin. I watched as she hopped out and hoisted a bulging backpack onto her broad shoulders. Even with her layers of outerwear and combat boots, I sensed she was athletic and strong.

"Well, it's our turn. Thank you, Kate." Dad opened his wallet and offered Kate a bit of cash. "For your trouble."

Kate blushed. "Aww, keep your money. It was a real pleasure meeting you. You both, I mean."

"Likewise. And if we need roadside assistance in the future, I know who to call," Dad joked, and opened the door.

A blast of cold rushed in. I groaned. Suddenly, I wanted to be anywhere else but here. My stomach loop-de-looped and my scarf bunched under my chin, scratchy and uncomfortable. I was not the girl to arrive on a motorbike during an epic snowstorm, though my mother would have. I was the quiet, introverted girl with the collection of Rubik's Cubes and vintage *Nancy Drew*s. The girl who had Mr. Safety First for a dad.

"Mills, what do you say to Kate?" Dad asked. So, Mr. Safety First was also Mr. Manners.

"Thank you." I forced a smile and took a deep breath before sliding out the door.

"Millie, wait." Kate reached into the console and pulled out a big bag of Twizzlers. "Making friends is easier with candy. Here, take it."

I looked at Kate and grinned. How was one lady so smart? "Wow. Thanks!"

"No problem, kiddo. Knock 'em dead."

"Millie!" Dad waved at me to hurry up.

I shoved the Twizzlers into my coat pocket. "Bye, Kate. I hope you get your flower shop."

Behind Dad, an elderly woman in thick-rimmed glasses pulled her green coat snug to block the cold. She looked too old to be out in this weather. Wasn't she worried about slipping or catching pneumonia? Maybe she was related to the Earharts and sent to welcome us. With all the giggling and gawking, a warm welcome would feel nice. But when your dad travels with a manikin and your passion is solving puzzles, you come to expect being frozen out. Sigh. That doesn't make the cold sting any less.

Still, I avoided the girls' stares as I carefully climbed out of the New Horizons Poultry cab. Ice coated the semi's running boards, making them as slippery as snot. I wasn't about to fall flat on my face now. Not after arriving like that. I gave Kate one last wave and tromped through the snow to Dad. The mystery lady in the green coat stepped forward with the help of a wooden cane. Now that I was closer, I could see that her eyes were crinkled around the edges like a crackled cookie. Her silver hair was cropped short, showcasing sparkling bird-shaped earrings, and her ruby lips highlighted a silver tooth and wide smile.

"Welcome to Amelia Earhart's birthplace and museum! I'm Birdie, the resident caretaker. What a blustery day!"

I managed a polite smile. "Nice to meet you. I'm Millie. And this is my Dad, Miles, and his, um, CPR manikin."

"A pleasure."

"You'll have to forgive our tardiness. We had, as you can see, a bit of car trouble."

"Not to worry, Mr. Ashford. This time of year can be brutal for transportation or ambulation, if you're ancient like me." She chuckled and thwacked her cane in the snow. A puff of white powder shot into the air. "At least two neighbors extended vacations to dodge the storm, and a third is stuck in Denver. 'Tis the season."

"Well, thank you for hosting," said Dad. "Even if it is a ghost town."

"Absolutely. A little snow doesn't rattle me. Most of the guardians have already left, with the exception of the motorcyclists and the Lams. They are, shall we say, quite thorough." Birdie's gaze shifted to a family of three.

I glanced over to the smartly dressed couple and their daughter. The dad wore a buttoned-up peacoat and pressed charcoal slacks. His face bore a scowl as he typed furiously on his phone. The mother, with her sleek ponytail, high-heeled boots, and chic wrap, adjusted the knot in her daughter's scarf and fired off a list of orders. The girl, wearing a plum-colored wool coat and coordinating tall boots trimmed with fur, nodded a quick yes. Her shiny black hair, which was trimmed into a severe bob, bounced in rhythm. I caught her eye and smiled.

She frowned.

Yikes.

A soft sigh escaped Birdie's lips, but she recovered quickly with a smile. "City folk don't always warm up to the Midwest. Now, may I get you anything? A cup of hot tea? You are more than welcome to use the telephone to call for a tow."

Dad hefted Danni under his arm. "Thank you, but that won't be necessary. Kate kindly radioed for a tow truck to fetch my car. But I am curious about whether the Lams would give me a ride to the inn."

Birdie patted his arm. "Let's ask. And if they can't, my nephew Collin can take you." Then, looking at me, she grinned. "Shall we get going? Chef Perry is preparing dinner, and we don't want to be late."

My stomach woke at the mention of food. "Sure," I replied, giving Dad (and Danni, by default) a quick hug. "Don't worry about me. I'll be fine. Promise." Though I said it as much for myself as for him.

Dad and I weren't great at good-byes or at being apart. It was one of the not-so-funny side effects of Mom's move. I was barely ten when she left. Ten when she showed us her career meant more to her than family. Dad broke down and bought me a phone, which helped, but I spent the next few months learning to live with anxiety. My heart pounded in my chest. My palms would sweat. My fingers clenched around my cube. Right. Left. Right. Deep breath. I wasn't solving; I was surviving.

And with counseling, I was doing okay, thank you very much. But I still missed her. The old version.

Every dang day.

Snowflakes dusted my face, and Dad chuckled. "I'll always worry about you, Mills. I'm your dad. It's what I do best. Remember, I'm a call away." And he planted a kiss on the top of my head. "See you first thing tomorrow."

"Tomorrow," I repeated.

Then, with my duffel bag thump-thumping against my leg, I followed Birdie down a snowy brick path toward Amelia's house. If Mom were here, she'd say this was a tip-top day. I should feel lucky to spend it with other smart girls. So why did I feel like I was plunging headfirst into choppy, cold waters teeming with hungry sharks?

CHAPTER THREE

"Girls!" Birdie shouted, and clapped twice. "Gather your things and head inside. You are in for a treat."

The others chatted excitedly as they collected their overnight bags and pillows. I noticed straightaway that two of them looked strikingly similar. And familiar. That's one side effect of reading mysteries like *Nancy Drew*. You get really good at noticing things other people miss. For instance, each girl had blond hair, only one's was swept into a topknot while the other's was cropped short with a flash of hot pink in the front. I wished I was that brave. That confident.

I had Ginny Weasley hair—straight, strawberry-colored, and awkwardly pinned on one side. In my morning rush, I'd thrown my warmest thermal on inside out. My galaxy hightops should make up for that. My toes touched the tips now, but I didn't care. I'd wear these kicks until they fell apart or aliens appeared. The laces glowed in the dark.

But these girls had style. Topknot dressed in tall, laced boots and trendy glasses, while Cool Hair wore ripped jeans and what could be described only as moon boots. Both girls had the same gray eyes, the same dimpled chin; they even had the same stance, putting all their weight on their left foot. They probably never tripped walking into a room or struggled to find glasses that would stay put on their noses.

Cool Hair pulled her phone out and started videoing. They had to be sisters. I knew I'd seen them before, maybe at a cubing event.

"Follow me. Don't be shy," Birdie called as she entered the dim hallway. "Come in, come in, there's enough room for everyone. Just stop at the stairs."

I stomped snow off my shoes and shuffled inside. My stomach fluttered with excitement. No, that's a lie. It fluttered with nerves. I was running on pure adrenaline and was clumped shoulder to shoulder with these girls like a bunch of huddled ducks. I took a deep breath and tried to act calm. *This will be fine. You will be fine.*

But I wasn't feeling fine. I was growing warmer by the second.

I unzipped my jacket, unwound my scarf, and elbowed Motorcycle Girl in the process. Now that her helmet was off,

I could see that she had flawless dark skin and killer corkscrew curls.

Sorry, I mouthed. *Close quarters.*

"Too close." The girl glanced at her watch and frowned. She had quite a collection of friendship bracelets. It must be nice to have so many friends.

Heat burned in my cheeks. Why did I have to be so awkward and anxious? I tucked my hair behind my ear and looked away.

Way to make friends, Millie. First the Lams' daughter, now Motorcycle Girl. This is why all your friends are either online or characters in books.

I decided to focus on my breathing and new surroundings. I would need to remember every detail for whenever I saw Mom next. Plus, it's always a good idea to note the exits in case of an emergency. Welcome to my brain.

Warm light bathed the entry, and a tapestry rug covered the sagging mahogany stairs. Fresh pine and cheery red ribbon wrapped the staircase's gleaming banister, making the foyer feel and smell like Christmas—and a hint of furniture polish. It was charming and festive and *oh my word*, straight out of a murder mystery.

I'd read online the home was built in 1861. And I knew from fourth-grade history that that year marked the start of the Civil War. Talk about ghosts. This house had stories, if not spooky spirits.

"I can't believe I'm here," Motorcycle Girl said behind me. She propped her motorcycle goggles on top of her head and loosened the scarf around her neck. With her leather coat and boots, she looked like a real aviatrix. "Amelia's house."

"You mean the middle of nowhere. There's no security guard or anything! Just a buzzer on a storm door. What kind of a museum is this?" The Lams' daughter, who'd frowned at me earlier, scowled.

"Midwesterners are known for being friendly and nice," I said.

Motorcycle Girl grinned. "And great at introductions."

I laughed and craned my neck for a better look at the cozy space, careful to not jab her in the ribs again. On my left, there was a wide doorway to what looked like a small library. A walnut table blocked the window, and two floor-to-ceiling cases were stuffed with books. A holiday tree filled the corner. Along the far wall, a fire burned in a black marbled hearth. The giant mirror over the mantel, easily one hundred years old, was guaranteed to bring seven years of bad luck if broken. There was an upright piano, too, and an enormous oil painting of a woman dressed in mourning clothes. Her bun was pulled so high and tight, she must have had a raging migraine. She also kind of gave me the creeps. "It's amazing and eerie all at once. Like the rooms have frozen in time."

"Exactly," Motorcycle Girl whispered. "Like a photograph."

"From the 1930s."

"Right." She nodded, and her hair boinged like a billion brass springs. "My name's Thea, by the way. Thea Cooke. What's yours?"

"Millie Ashford," I whispered back. "Nice to meet you."

Thea paused for a nanosecond, then asked, "Well, Millie Ashford, do you believe in ghosts?"

"Ghosts?" The Lam girl turned her head and scoffed. "There's no such thing as ghosts."

"Maybe." I shrugged. "Though considering the tragic way the former resident met her demise, and seeing as how the home was built in 1861, is stuffed with antiques, *and* sits across the street from a hazardous bluff overlooking a rapid river, I'm pretty sure this place would make a perfect haunt."

The girl rolled her eyes and adjusted the leather strap of her overnight bag cutting into her shoulder. Of course the bag was monogrammed with her initial, *C*. Quite possibly stitched in unicorn hair. I made a game of trying to guess her name. Cate? Caroline? No, too sweet.

Carly?

"Cassandra, as I was saying . . ." Birdie rapped her cane against the hardwood floor. "I'd like to be the first to—"

Cassandra brushed her straight black bangs out of her eyes and raised her hand to get Birdie's attention. "It's Cassie. Thanks."

"Cassie. Of course." Birdie smiled and started again.

"Girls, I'd like to be the first to welcome you to Judge Alfred and Amelia Otis's home, the birthplace of Amelia Earhart, American aviation pioneer and first female to fly solo across the Atlantic Ocean. I'm Birdie Anderson, the museum's resident caretaker. We are going to have a fabulous time. Please relax and make yourselves at home."

Relax. Yeah, right. I was far too excited to relax. I looked over at Thea, snapping pictures of the ceiling while Birdie continued:

"Chef Perry is in the kitchen, and my fabulous housekeeper, Edna, is tidying the upstairs. Then there's Ms. Hegg, head of the Ninety-Nines and sender of your invitations. She so hoped to be here tonight to greet you all but is delayed due to weather. But back to the house itself. Can anyone tell me who the Otises were and why Amelia was born here?"

A girl in the front, wearing a thick braid and striped leggings, raised her hand. A galaxy of freckles dusted her brown face, and her eyes sparkled like stars. Environmental patches—EARTH DAY, SAVE THE WHALES, and GEOLOGY ROCKS!—covered her tote bag. "The Otises were Amelia's maternal grandparents, and Amelia's mom lived at home before she gave birth."

Birdie smiled. "Well done! Thank you, Nathalie."

Nathalie beamed like she'd just won one hundred tickets at Skee-Ball. I loved Skee-Ball, almost as much as cubing, or skateboarding, or cubing while skateboarding. Dad called that a fast pass to the emergency room, but so far, I'd been lucky.

Birdie continued, "Amelia's father, a lawyer and claims agent for the railroad, traveled often for work, and the Otises felt that their daughter would have a safer pregnancy and delivery at home. So, Amy Otis Earhart returned to her parents' house here on the bluff, and on July twenty-fourth, 1897, she gave birth to Amelia."

Nathalie's hand shot back in the air. "What about Amelia's flight goggles? Will we get to see them?"

"Achoo!" Topknot sneezed.

"Bless you," I whispered, and she gave me a grateful smile.

"I thought you'd never ask!" Birdie said over us. "Let's do a quick tour, as you'll have all night to explore. Now, if you'll please pay attention, I will show you the downstairs. It's mazelike, but no one's gone missing yet."

"Famous last words," Thea muttered.

I giggled. I liked Thea already. Cassandra/Cassie, not so much.

Birdie prattled on. "To your left we have the Otises' small library, with our own aviation-themed tree. The many airplane ornaments are gifts from fans." Birdie paused for us to take in the view. "Amelia and her sister, Muriel, spent the happiest parts of their childhood here with their grandparents, no doubt reading many great books in front of the fire. In addition to being a judge, Alfred Otis served as president of

Atchison Savings Bank, so the girls were doted upon. Though their grandmother disapproved of Amelia's free spirit. She was always scolding her for unladylike activities like hopping fences, sledding on her belly, and shooting rats in the barn with her shotgun."

Rats. I shuddered. I hated rats. I'd shoot them too. Though I'd have to use a slingshot, as Dad had a strict no-firearms policy.

"Achoo." The same girl sneezed again.

"And on the other side of the gold drapes, a special surprise waits for you in the reading room. . . . Oh!" Birdie stopped. "There you are, you fat cat. You're always getting under my feet." Birdie stooped to scoop up a plump kitten. "Everyone, meet Electra. She would like me to remind you that this is her house too. So please treat it with care and respect."

"She's beautiful," Thea said. I agreed, even though dogs were my favorite. But Electra's charcoal coat and yellow-green eyes were hard to miss. They stood in contrast to a milky patch of fur that streaked from her forehead down her nose like lightning.

"Beautiful and bossy," said Birdie, setting her down. "She's also named for something related to Amelia. Any guesses?"

"This one's easy," whispered Nathalie.

"An airplane," the girl with pink hair said from behind her phone. She was still recording. I hoped she brought her charger.

"Yes. Exactly. Amelia was flying her all-metal, twin-engine Lockheed Model 10-E Electra when she disappeared. You'll find a model replica I built in the sunroom, just past the reading room. Now, back down this main hall is the butler's pantry, behind the stairs to your right, and straight ahead is the old kitchen, now a gift shop, with entry into the formal dining room. That is where we will have our evening meal."

On cue, my stomach growled. I tried to sneak a peek through the gift shop into the dining room, but Birdie was giving us a flyby view, not a full tour. Like she said, we had all night to explore.

"I don't know about you, but I'm hungry," Thea whispered. I started to reply that I felt the same way, until I remembered the bag of candy from Kate.

"Twizzler?" I asked, holding them out.

Thea's eyes lit up as she pulled out a stick of licorice. "Yes. Thanks."

"No problem," I said, and immediately sensed someone eavesdropping on our conversation. "Would you like one, Cassie?"

Cassie snorted. "Artificial colors and preservatives? Gross."

"Suit yourself," I said, and bit into a sugary red rope. Strawberry flavoring exploded inside my mouth, and I smiled. Kate was right.

Candy *was* great for making friends.

CHAPTER FOUR

Meanwhile, Birdie kept on. "And if you look across the entryway from the library, you'll see the judge's parlor— where the men of the home would gather to have a cigar. This room flows into the butler's pantry and breezeway. The Otises had five children, and after the birth of each, they built on a new wing. So, the house grew and expanded with the family. Oh, and the carriage house is out back, but of course the weather has hampered that much of our tour." Birdie caught her breath. "But let's head upstairs. You have about fifteen minutes to choose a bed, unpack, use the facilities— second door on the left—and meet me back here. Chef Perry has prepared a wonderful welcome dinner. Cassandra—I mean, *Cassie*, will you kindly lead the way upstairs?"

The girls blocking the grand staircase shuffled aside

while Cassie made a big to-do of lugging her bag behind her.

"She probably has a butler carry her luggage at home," whispered Thea.

I grinned. But to Cassie's credit, she carried her bag all the way up.

I hitched my bag onto my shoulder once more and followed the stream of girls up the stairs. The wall was lined with photographs of Amelia, as well as a pair of crossed swords.

Thea pointed to them and nudged me. "Amelia was a fencing coach."

"Ha! I bet." I laughed.

"No, really. I'm not making it up." Thea stopped beneath the blades. "When Amelia was a social worker in Boston, she taught dozens of Chinese and Syrian kids how to play basketball and fence."

"No way!" I said. "She's even cooler than I thought."

"Totally." Thea smiled. "Humans are like cake. We have layers."

"Layers. I like that." My Rubik's Cube had layers. Funny how a few twists and turns make the most basic shape complex.

At the top of the landing, a door marked STAFF ONLY greeted me.

"That's my quarters straight ahead," Birdie said, leaning on her cane. "Forgive me for not climbing the stairs with you. It's tiring for old bones like mine to take too many trips up and down in one day. I've lived here close to thirty-five years, and I don't see a reason to move my bedroom just yet."

I could hear the others chattering down the hall, their overnight bags rolling with reverberating thumps along the floorboards.

Birdie's voice grew louder, carrying up the staircase. "The first bedroom to your right, that was Amelia's mother's, Amy Otis Earhart's, room, the very room in which Amelia was born. Two of you can share the queen bed, and, of course, there is plenty of space on the floor for a couple of sleeping bags, or there's the guest bedroom on the opposite side of the hall. The only closed rooms are mine and Amelia's. Hers is at the end of the hall and overlooks the front of the house. It's roped off for now."

My heart sank. I'd really hoped to go into Amelia's childhood bedroom.

Chin up, Millie. You're still one of six girls chosen to stay the night.

I reached the top of the stairs as Cassie neared the end of the hall. The two lookalikes raced to claim Amy Otis Earhart's room. I wasn't going to have much choice, being the last one up, so I let the others fight it out while I soaked in my surroundings. The upper hallway looked more like an elongated sitting room, with a sprinkling of furniture and a pair of arched French doors at the end.

The last rays of daylight filtered in through the doors' brilliant stained glass, painting colorful splashes of light across the floor. Maybe in nice weather, Amelia and her sister walked out onto the small balcony to watch the trains chug across the railway bridge over the Missouri River below. Or maybe they read stacks of books on a plush velvet sofa similar to the one in front of me now.

Anyway, I needed to hurry up if I was going to claim a sleeping spot. So, I pushed on the door to my left. It swung open, and I flicked on the light.

And jumped.

My heart caught in my throat. My muscles tensed.

I hadn't found a bedroom. What I'd stumbled upon looked more like an amazing exhibit of Madame Tussauds wax figures. Imagine a bunch of mannequins throwing a surprise party, only the surprise was on me. (As an aside, medical manikins are spelled one way. Department store mannequins are spelled another.) There was a flight suit and cap, an old-fashioned deep-sea diving outfit, two evening gowns, a simple navy dress with a wide sailor collar, and a form-fitting dress with tailored slacks, a blouse, and a coordinating silk scarf. Each mannequin was artfully posed and illuminated by its own spotlight. I put my hand over my mouth to stifle a laugh. I'd jumped out of my skin over a bunch of sharply dressed mannequins.

I started to close the door, but a glass display case in the center of the room caught my attention. Now, normally I wouldn't have looked twice, but, well, Kate *had* just mentioned the news about the Smithsonian wanting Amelia's goggles, and, well . . . I made my first mistake of the night.

I tiptoed up to the glass.

CHAPTER FIVE

A shiny brass plaque confirmed what I was thinking: FLIGHT GOGGLES WORN BY AMELIA EARHART ON HER SOLO FLIGHT ACROSS THE ATLANTIC ON MAY 20–21, 1932.

"Whoa." I leaned so close that my breath fogged up the glass.

The leather straps looked old and cracked. My brain fired a million neurons. Was I really staring at Amelia Earhart's goggles? The ones she wore on her solo flight across the Atlantic Ocean. The ones worth $120,000. The ones quite possibly going to the Smithsonian National Air and Space Museum in *Washington, DC*. My fingers itched to touch the metal frames, the worn leather, the honey-yellow lenses peeking through thick lines of tape. I wondered what the tape was for and if these were her favorite pair. Surely the great Amelia had more than one pair of flight goggles. She probably had dozens and a sponsor, like athletes do today. Speedo for swimmers. Nike for runners. Who made flight attire? Mom would know.

My duffel's strap dug into my shoulder.

Mom. She'd never believe this.

I couldn't wait to tell her I saw Amelia's goggles with my own eyes, along with an actual, signed note. I squinted to read the fading type on yellowed paper.

Dear Mr. Fernstrom:

Thank you for taking the trouble to return my goggles. I appreciate your courtesy very much. That particular pair are rather historic. Also they have grown accustomed to me, and cling around my unconventional nose more effectively than new ones.

Sincerely yours,

Amelia Earhart

Wow! So her goggles had gone missing, and this Mr. Fernstrom must have found them. That's pretty awesome, if you ask me. Not to mention they were the aviatrix's favorite pair, as they fit her "unconventional" nose. I smiled. Amelia thought her nose was unusual. Maybe she wasn't so different from me.

"You!" a voice barked.

I jumped for the second time that night.

"What are you doing in here?" A short woman in a housekeeper's uniform blocked the doorway. Her hands were glued to her hips, and her round face was flushed purple. "This room is off-limits until Birdie says otherwise."

"Oh," I said. "I . . . I was looking for a place to sleep, and . . ."

"Well, you won't find any beds in here," she huffed. "Out!"

I nodded and quickly shuffled past her into the hallway. I caught a whiff of peppermint breath as she jangled some keys and ranted: "How am I supposed to work surrounded by all these girls?"

I hoped right then and there I didn't have to see this lady for the rest of the night.

I darted into Amelia's mother's room across the hall, where the two blond girls introduced themselves as Robin and Wren Winters. Sisters. I knew it. They'd already claimed the queen-size bed at the far end of the room and tossed their overcoats onto the floor too. Wren, the one with bright pink highlights, had sunk into a huge cane rocking chair and kicked off her moon boots. Talk about making oneself at home. Ha.

I was about to ask if they had an extra pillow when Wren whipped her smartphone from her pocket and frowned. "No signal. Great. I told you we'd have better service on Mars than here."

That's when it all came together. I *had* seen these girls before. They were the twins who ran the popular Mars Millennium website and had approximately a gazillion and one-half followers. The Mars Millen was an organization by and for teens who hoped to be the first people to colonize the planet Mars. And the Winterses were legitimate stars. They even won an international naming competition for the new rover and took their viewers on a tour of NASA's Jet Propulsion Lab in Pasadena, California. Mr. Salmon, my science teacher, sometimes streamed their interviews of famous astronauts and scientists at the end of class. I couldn't believe I hadn't clued in sooner to who they were. I debated telling them about the mannequin room across the hall, but I didn't want any more trouble.

"Eh, give it a rest, Wren, and enjoy the moment. We can record later." Robin, the one with the topknot, turned her attention from reading plaques tacked to the wall to inspecting a wooden trunk by her feet. She blew a thin layer of dust off the top and squealed in surprise.

"Wow! This is Amelia's hope chest."

"Hope what?" asked Wren.

"Hope chest," Robin replied. "Like the antique trunk Grandma had in her attic that once belonged to her mother. Don't you remember her saying that brides used to fill these heirloom trunks with linens and dishes and candles—anything they would need as new brides?"

Wren grunted. "That is so sexist. What about guys? Did *they* get chests filled with tools, boots, and suspenders?"

I smiled and dropped my bag to the floor. "Don't forget long underwear and a shaving kit."

"No, wait. Beard oil!" Wren giggled. "For when your beard needs one hundred percent more grease."

"Or mustache wax! To get those curlicue tips," I said with a laugh.

"Well, whether you are for or against hope chests, you are welcome to stay in Amy Otis's room with us. Nathalie's gone to get her sleeping bag, but there's still plenty of space."

Nathalie. The smart one who asked about the goggles.

Robin's eyes danced as she motioned to a pile of pillows and quilts. "Do you think this is the bed Amelia was born in?"

"Birdie would know. We could ask her." I slipped my cube from my jacket pocket and started solving. Maybe I should at least warn them about the angry maid. What did Birdie say her name was? Ella?

Wren rolled her eyes. "Please. I can't believe Birdie is in charge of us all night. We'll have to come up with something, or this whole night will be one big bore."

"Boring? How can you even call spending the night in Amelia's house 'boring'?" Robin flopped back on the bed, which Amelia may or may not have been birthed in, and gave a contented sigh. "Amelia dreamt here. Gazed beyond the windowpane. To the waiting sky."

"Another haiku. You are hopeless." Wren spiked her hair in Amy Otis's mirror and sighed. "My sister is leading an arts initiative to launch a book of poetry into space."

Robin grinned. "That's why you love me. But think about it, Wren. Maybe little Amelia was sent to time out in this very corner, in *your* rocking chair."

Wren snorted. "You're such a sap."

Sisters. I smiled to myself and started a new solve.

"I hope you don't solve that thing in your sleep," Wren said, pointing to my flying fingers. "Because I need to catch my z's, or I will be a total beast."

My fingers stilled, and my smile stuck like superglue.

Robin propped herself up on her elbow and rolled her eyes. "It's true. She can be a complete bear, but don't worry. You're still welcome to sleep here. Wren travels with earplugs."

"Er. Thanks," I replied, suddenly feeling very out of place. "I think I'll check out the other room and find Amelia's, too, even if we can't go in. I mean, that's why we're here, right? To see her house?" I shrugged and tucked my cube back into my pocket for safekeeping.

Ugh. Why did I have to be so awkward? There's nothing wrong with cubing. Nothing. Or spontaneous haikus. I liked Robin. Wren? Maybe she'd grow on me.

"Well, you know where to find us," Robin said, back to staring at a crack in the ceiling.

I sighed. Even Twizzlers couldn't help me now, so I picked up my bag and trudged into the hallway. But something hanging on the wall outside stopped me in my tracks.

Amelia's handprint. Framed.

The page was actually signed *Amelia Earhart* and dated by the pilot on June 28, 1933. Four years before she disappeared.

Goose bumps tickled my arms as I placed my left hand on the glass over Amelia's inked one. What was the Amelia quote Mom used to say?

"A single act of kindness throws out roots in all directions . . ." I began.

"And the roots spring up and make new trees."

I turned to see who had finished the quote and was surprised to find the girl in the striped leggings sprawled on the hardwood floor. She'd ducked her head and shoulders underneath the antique chaise longue, like she was searching for something.

"It's a misattribution," her voice floated up.

"You must be Nathalie." I crept closer, curious why this girl was underneath the sofa. "And . . . what's a 'misattribution'?"

"That quote. Amelia didn't really say that. Well, she did, but she was quoting an old British guy, some theologian named Faber." The girl slid out and bonked her head on the furniture. "*Ow.*"

I winced. "Have you lost something?"

Nathalie groaned. "Not something. Some*one*. Rosie Stancer."

"Oh." I bit my lip, confused. "You've lost the famous polar explorer?"

Nathalie stood and brushed a strand of hair out of her eyes. "No, silly. Rosie Stancer . . . my pet rat."

CHAPTER SIX

Like I said, if there was one thing I did not do, it was rats. "Your pet rat."

Nathalie's eyes welled. "*Yes*. My pet rat. And she's got to be so frightened to be in a new place, and now she's all alone. She's not brave like the Arctic explorer at all. She's quite the opposite, really. She'd die before she gnawed off her own frostbitten toe."

I shuddered. "Okay. What does she look like? Your Rosie, I mean." I could not even believe I was asking such a horrid question. I liked rats as much as dogs liked cats.

Nathalie took a shaky breath. "White. Stark white with a teensy black heart behind her left ear. And the cutest pink ears and—"

A shriek tore across the hallway.

Nathalie and I rushed toward the noise.

Quilted twin beds, separated by single night table, took up the bulk of the guest room. Thea sat on one bed, calmly unpacking. But standing on top of the other bed, hopping from one foot to the other, was Cassie.

"He's under the dresser! No, the dresser! Get him! Get *him*!"

I wanted to laugh at how ridiculous she looked, but part of me wanted to join her. We actually had something in common: a hatred for rodents.

Nathalie's voice turned stern. "Rosie's a *she*. And if you expect me to retrieve her from your room, you must calm down. You are scaring her."

Cassie's mouth snapped shut, though her eyes could still kill. Satisfied, Nathalie crouched beside the dresser in an attempt to coax out her pet.

"Here, Rosie. Come on, girl. I've brought you a treat."

From my safe spot in the doorway, I surveyed the room. The antique dresser, under which Rosie Stancer was hiding, held a round makeup mirror and a stack of well-worn books. The top title was a biography of Amelia; I knew it by the giant photograph. In fact, all the photos in the room were of Amelia. Amelia with her Lockheed Vega, which she called her "Little Red Bus." Amelia in full diving gear. Amelia riding a scooter. Amelia holding a huge bouquet of roses and waving to an enormous crowd.

"Got her!" Nathalie stood up, cupping Rosie Stancer between her hands. "Aww. You're such a good girl too. You brought me a present!"

Now, this I had to see. Rosie Stancer's rosy nose sniffed the air. Her whiskers twitched, but it was her two front feet that got my attention. They held a shiny penny.

Thea's eyes grew wide. "Does she always bring you money?"

Nathalie laughed. "I trained her to bring me coins, so if we are out and she finds one, yes." She turned to her pet. "Good job, Rosie. Now, stay put." Nathalie kissed Rosie's furry head, then dropped her inside her jacket pocket.

"You carry her in your pocket?" I asked.

Nathalie beamed. "Oh, sure. She's very laid back. Someone"—she glanced at Cassie—"must have spooked her to make her run wild."

"Birdie has a cat, remember? Maybe she sensed a *predator*." Cassie sat like a pretzel on the bed and hugged her monogrammed pillow to her chest. Of course she traveled with her own monogrammed pillow.

Thea rolled her eyes and moved huge headphones from her suitcase to the nightstand.

"Electra won't be a problem. Will she, Rosie?" Nathalie scratched behind her pet's ears. "Rosie will be with me or in her box, on the dresser. Out of the way and safe."

I plopped my bag down next to Thea's, as the only place

left for me was right here on the floor. "Well, it's not every day you get the chance to spend the night in Amelia Earhart's house." So help me, I was tired of talking about rats, even the friendly kind.

"True." Natalie smiled. "It seems like a dream, doesn't it? I can't wait to call my mom in a bit."

"Must be nice. My mother won't leave me alone." Cassie dug through her overnight bag and pulled out a round tin.

I smiled, but on the inside, my heart ached. I wished my mom called. I wished she nagged me so much it was irritating. Instinctively, I reached for Mom's pin. Funny how Kate had seemed more interested in my life than my own mother was.

Cassie lifted the lid to reveal what could only be a pile of dried seaweed nestled inside crinkly tissue paper. I wrinkled my nose.

"Kale chips," she said. Then she picked the tissue paper up by the edges and tossed it, chips and all, in the trash.

I gasped.

But there was another layer of tissue in the bottom of the tin.

A big grin spread across Cassie's face as she peeled back the paper. "Anyone care for a brownie? They're out of this world." She tore open a vacuum-sealed square and inhaled its sweet scent. "I swiped a few from NASA." She took a bite and sighed. "Perfection."

"Cool." Thea reached for one.

My mouth watered, but I held back. I didn't trust Cassie quite yet. "What do you mean you 'swiped' them?"

Cassie popped another brownie into her mouth. "Have you ever sneaked anything before?"

A knock sounded at the door, and the housekeeper poked her head in. She had a feather duster in her hand and didn't look too chipper about it. "Birdie asks everyone to join her in the dining room." She glared at me. "Now."

Nathalie shrugged. "Guess we'd better hurry downstairs." Then she patted her pocket and whispered so only I could hear, "I hope there's something at dinner for Rosie. She can be such a picky eater when we travel."

CHAPTER SEVEN

We made our way downstairs and slipped past the small gift shop, which was bursting with posters and maps and books. There would be time to browse later. For now, dinner called.

The temperature dropped as we squeezed through an enclosed breezeway to reach the Otises' oval dining room. It was Old World fancy. A brass chandelier hung beneath a colorful ceiling medallion. The walls were painted deep cranberry, and thick trim outlined the high, arched windows. But the best part was the center panes. They contained squares of stained glass, which looked a lot like my Rubik's Cube.

Of course, Edna, the grouchy housekeeper I'd met upstairs, had the table meticulously set. Fine white dishes, fanned napkins, and gleaming flatware decorated each place setting, along with mini cans of what looked like soup. Cute. In the middle of the table sat gigantic platters heaped with garlic chicken, roasted root vegetables, and buttery home- made rolls. Yum. One bowl was filled with hard-boiled eggs. Another with applesauce. I hadn't seen this much food at one meal since Thanksgiving at Grandma Ashford's.

"This looks and smells incredible," I said.

"Tell me about it," Thea said, and patted her stomach. "I can't wait to dig in."

Wren pulled out a chair. "Me neither."

I didn't know where to sit, so I chose a seat near the kitchen, next to Nathalie. She was already breaking apart fancy geometric crackers and smuggling the crumbs under- neath the table to Rosie. Meanwhile, Cassie plucked a bright red flower from the vase, sniffed it, and tucked it behind her ear before claiming the chair to my right. Once everyone was seated, Birdie picked up her glass of ice water and clinked her spoon against the side.

"Girls, welcome to the Otis family's dining room. This is Chef Perry. He's in charge of the food and has been working here for two months—ever since the Ninety-Nines decided I was too old and frail to fry myself an egg." Birdie laughed at her own joke.

I looked at Nathalie, who shrugged.

Chef Perry, wearing a crisp white uniform and neatly trimmed beard, shook his head and grinned. "Don't listen to her. Ms. Birdie can fry an egg like no one's business. The Ninety-Nines were simply being cautious in hiring me."

Pleased by the praise, Birdie blushed. "Chef Perry's saving up for school. He's been accepted to the prestigious Culinary Institute of America. Though I don't know what else they can possibly teach him. He's already worked at the White House!"

Wow. Nathalie's mouth dropped open in awe.

Perry laughed and changed the subject. "Judging a cookie contest is hardly working. May I tell our guests about tonight's menu?"

Birdie sat up. "Yes, but first I should explain. In case you didn't know, the Ninety-Nines is the first group of international women pilots. They own and manage this historic site. They also helped sponsor your event tonight, so you wouldn't be here if not for them, NASA, and Girls in Science. They are an extraordinary group of women. Does anyone happen to know what year the Ninety-Nines were founded?"

"Nineteen twenty-nine?" Cassie guessed.

"Bingo." Birdie beamed and tossed Cassie a Hershey's Kiss. "Now, who can tell me the name of their first president?"

Thea raised her hand. "Amelia Earhart!"

"Right again!" Birdie threw a chocolate to Thea. "And who can name one fact about Amelia Earhart?"

"In 1932, she became the first woman to fly solo across the Atlantic Ocean."

"Well done, Wren. You all are going to love the game."

Wren popped a candy into her mouth while my stomach flopped. Game? What game? But before I could dwell on the possibilities, Chef Perry cleared his throat. "Thank you, Birdie. I know everyone is famished from traveling, so I'll be quick. Birdie and I have combed through dozens of old cookbooks and Earhart family recipes in order to prepare Amelia's favorite dishes just for you. You'll notice cans of tomato juice next to your ice water. Amelia loved tomato juice and took some, along with raisins, hard-boiled eggs, or pieces of dark chocolate with her on flights. She'd open the cans with an ice pick, but we've gone ahead and done that part for you."

"Safety first," Wren mumbled, looking disappointed.

Perry laughed. "Always. Now that you know this, the next time you fly, you can ask for tomato juice in honor of Amelia."

Wren shrugged. "Okay."

Perry smiled. "Back to the menu. We know Amelia liked her mother's fried chicken, but she often requested garlic chicken as an adult. So that's what I've made tonight. Pan-roasted chicken smothered in a creamy garlic sauce with a hearty side of roasted fingerling potatoes and carrots, finished with a citrus salad and homemade yeast rolls. And please save room for dessert! It's her very favorite, second only to blueberry ice cream, which is sadly out of season."

Chef Perry clasped his hands together and grinned. As he did so, his sleeve shifted on his forearm, revealing a series of tattoos. I loved tattoos and was somewhat obsessed with them.

I took a sip of my tomato juice and studied Chef Perry's arm. The first tattoo was some sort of a root vegetable, maybe a rutabaga. Or a turnip. Then there was a chef's knife, followed by a big fork. But the last tattoo didn't fit the food theme: It looked like an airplane. Yes, most definitely an airplane. That was an interesting choice for a chef. But before I could analyze his ink any further, Birdie piped up.

"Thank you, Perry. It looks delicious."

"You're most welcome. If you'll excuse me, I need to attend to a small matter in the kitchen." Turning to Birdie, he added, "Your nephew called and is on his way."

Birdie looked out the window at the blowing snow and sighed. "Thank you. Though I can't believe he agreed to come in this weather. He rarely visits when it is eighty and sunny."

Perry smiled as he exited the room. "You can't blame him for wanting a good meal, Birdie."

"A free meal is more like it!" she muttered. "Now, girls, don't be shy. I'm surely not! Go on, eat!"

For the next few moments all anyone could hear was the clattering of utensils on plates. Chef Perry was an honest-to-goodness kitchen magician. The meal was beyond good; even the cooked carrots, which have never been my favorite, disappeared from my plate. In fact, I was chewing the last one when the wind howled through the trees outside and killed the lights.

I stopped chewing.

Forks froze.

The room was as dark as midnight, save for the screen on Wren's phone.

"Everyone remain calm," Birdie said. "I'm sure it's only temporary." Then, voilà! The lights flipped back on.

I swallowed the last bite of carrot and laughed with relief. It can be spooky at home when the power goes out, but staying the night in a dark, cold, Civil War–era mansion? No thank you.

"We won't lose power for good, will we?" Thea asked, her eyes huge.

"Worse things have happened, my dear. But my nephew is bringing extra firewood, just in case. We'll be plenty warm. And your guardians are only a call away at the Atchison Inn. But enough of that," she said, taking her napkin and dabbing her lips. "Why don't we go around the table and get to know one another a little better? Nathalie, will you start? Tell us your name and a fact or two about yourself. We'll go around clockwise and end with Millie."

Birdie beamed at us like a proud grandmother while Nathalie put down her potatoes and began.

"I'm Nathalie Ramirez. I'm eleven, like most of you. I'm

from Southern California and am fascinated with animals and female explorers. My mother is a zoologist currently stationed at Penguin Ranch in Cape Washington, Antarctica. I miss her, but I get to stay with my abuela while she's away. She's an amazing cook."

Wow. When Nathalie mentioned calling her mom, she meant all the way in Antarctica!

Wren leaned back and whistled. "Antarctica sounds amazing."

"Yeah." Nathalie grinned. "I hope to visit next year."

Ding-dong.

"Oh, bother. That's the door." The crease between Birdie's brows deepened. "Girls, continue without me. I'll be back momentarily."

Birdie excused herself from the table and disappeared into the kitchen. Electra ran after her, and Robin sneezed.

"Achoo!"

I hadn't noticed until this moment how red and puffy Robin's eyes looked. She must have been catching a cold.

"Well, I'm Wren Winters, and this is my sister, Robin. We're from snowy Minnesota. And as you can see, Robin's allergic to cats. I warned her old ladies *always* have cats. It's code: Slippers. Tea. Cats. Where are the old ladies with boots and pythons? That's what I want to know," Wren said, and stabbed a piece of chicken.

"I should never have picked up Electra." Robin blew her

nose into her napkin. "I love cats. They just don't love me."

"Well, you can't be in our video looking like you're on day two of the flu."

"What video?" Thea asked. "I didn't know there'd be a video."

"Oh, not an official one," Wren said. "One for our YouTube channel, the Mars Millennium. We'd promised our subscribers we would post a video about our weekend. Hmm. An interesting fact about us is that we are related to a charter member of the Ninety-Nines, Nellie Zabel Willhite. Nellie was the first female pilot in South Dakota and possibly the first licensed deaf pilot in the world."

"That's incredible!" I said.

"Isn't it?" said Wren. "She could sense engine trouble by a change in vibrations."

"Achoo!" Robin sneezed again.

"Bless you."

"Thank you. I have allergy medicine upstairs." Robin pushed back her chair.

"I'll run and get it," Cassie offered. "If you tell me where it is." *Huh*, I thought as she excused herself from the table. *That's the first nice thing she's said.*

"Thank you. That's so kind. It's in my toiletry kit inside my turquoise overnight bag. So, Thea, what are you into?" Robin asked.

Thea sat up, sending her bronze curls springing in all

directions. "I'm Thea Cooke, and I'm from Fort Worth, Texas. I come from a family of mechanical and computer engineers. We build model airplanes and cars for fun. My hero is Bessie Coleman, a stunt flyer and the first African American woman to earn a pilot's license. I like coding, tacos, and hip-hop, but not ghosts."

"We studied Bessie Coleman at school. She only performed in air shows if the crowds were desegregated, meaning everyone entered and enjoyed the show together, no matter their race," Nathalie said.

"True." Thea smiled. "Her mother was African American and her father Native American. She couldn't find a flight teacher because of her gender and skin color."

"So how did she learn to fly?" I asked.

"She studied French and applied to aviation schools in Europe instead."

Robin clapped. "*Magnifique.*"

Thea nodded. "Bessie came back to the US and flew borrowed planes until she'd saved enough money to buy her own. Then, right after she made her final payment, her plane malfunctioned during a practice flight."

"Oh no," Robin said. "What happened?"

"She fell out of the open cockpit to her death."

"How horrible." Nathalie set her tomato juice down.

"Well, that stinks," Wren added.

"Totally. She was only thirty-four, but," Thea continued,

"she paved the way for countless pilots of color, including my grandfather."

Thea then told us about the robots she's building—an automatic cat feeder, a sweeper, and a high-tech prosthetic—plus the motorcycle sidecar she and her auntie had restored. She'd rewired the bike herself.

"Is that the rusty contraption you arrived in?" Cassie asked, back with the medicine.

"Yes," Thea replied. "Though she prefers 'vintage' to 'rusty' and loves when you use her royal name, Queen Beth."

Liking Thea was a no-brainer, but Cassie was up next. Everyone waited patiently for her to finish chewing a bite of chicken.

"As you know, I'm Cassie Lam," she began. "I'm from Houston, Texas, and I've been to Space Camp three years in a row. Though it's not anything like the *real* Space Center, it's still pretty cool. My mom works at NASA. She's the director of food science and their top food engineer, with high-level clearance. She helps develop the menus for those on board the ISS, the International Space Station. I'm a foodie, so sometimes she lets me sample new recipes from the test kitchen." She looked at me. "The brownies I brought are one of the few food items—along with nuts, candy, crackers—sent into orbit as NF. In their natural form. They're not dehydrated, freeze-dried, or irradiated." Cassie paused. "This is why my family's Space Farming Initiative is so important. If humans hope to colonize Mars, we will need the ability to grow crops effectively in zero gravity. Right now we're perfecting an inflatable greenhouse." She nodded her head once and smiled like she'd given a speech to announce her candidacy for president.

Meanwhile, my stomach twisted into knots. I could have sworn someone cranked the heat up. I wiped my sweaty palms on my napkin.

"What about you, Millie?" Cassie asked, and smiled a little too sweetly.

"What about me?" I asked, wanting to puke. "Uh. Well, I'm Millie Ashford, and I cube." It came out in a croak. "See?" I pulled my cube from my pocket and then stuffed it back out of sight. "I've won some awards. I can solve a three-by-three in under ten seconds. I can also do a one-handed solve, but of course that takes more time."

"Nice." Robin's smile stretched beneath her puffy eyes. "Where are you from? And didn't we see your dad with a ventriloquist's dummy?"

Everyone choked on their food, and heat rushed up my neck. "Oh, Kansas City at the moment. We . . . sort of move around." I swore my ears were on fire. "Dad's a CPR trainer, so he travels a lot, educating people around the Midwest on proper lifesaving technique. You saw Danni, his newest training manikin."

Cassie laughed. "So, you play with puzzles *and* dolls!

What are you doing at Amelia's house, then?"

"That's not what I meant," Robin said with a frown.

"It's okay," I said. "My mom's a pilot. She named me after Amelia, but I haven't seen her in a year. Actually, four hundred and thirty-three days. My mom, I mean. Not Amelia." I looked at my plate and willed myself to spontaneously combust. "I like science, mysteries, and math."

"And that's precisely why you are here, my dear!" Birdie said from the doorway. "Because you are curious about the world around you. That's true for each of you."

I gave her a grateful smile.

Birdie pushed her big glasses up onto her nose, and as she did so, her many bracelets clattered along her wiry arm. "I'd like for you to meet my no-good nephew, Collin, who stuffs animals in his parents' basement."

Nathalie's eyes grew round.

"Collin! Come say hello. These girls don't bite. At least, I don't think they do."

Birdie winked at us, and a man, older than Chef Perry but younger than Dad, appeared.

Collin had wild brown hair and a beard. He wore a wrinkled flannel shirt, and his jeans were faded, rolled at the cuff. Black-and-gold socks peered over the tops of tan boots he hadn't bothered to lace.

"Hello," he said, like he'd rather be anywhere but here. "You girls are the cream of the crop, eh?" He cocked his head to one side and scratched his stomach like he'd just woken up. Maybe he had.

I wasn't sure why Birdie was so hard on him, even though I knew from personal experience that family could be tricky. Then he plucked one of her chocolates off the table without even asking or unwrapping it (a minor detail) and popped the entire piece into his mouth. And chewed.

I gagged.

Collin laughed at my reaction, then helped himself to a plate he piled high with Amelia's favorite food. "I'm as hungry as the last bobcat I stuffed."

Wren snorted. "You're a taxidermist."

"That's right. No job's too hard or too small for me. I've prepped all kinds of creatures, from six-foot Louisiana gators down to tiny pocket pets. Mice are my specialty."

Nathalie let out a yelp, and Collin pierced a piece of chicken with his fork. "But the bigger the better, I always say. Where is old Electra, anyway?" He grinned.

Robin's face grew pale, and I pushed my plate away. As much as I hated rodents, the thought of anyone's pet, especially Birdie's beloved cat, being stuffed and mounted like a museum trophy made me sick.

"That's quite enough, Collin," Birdie snapped.

"Aww. I'm just messing with them, Aunt Birdie. You know I only work on specimens who've died from natural causes. Like this delicious bird." He winked and shoved another piece of garlic chicken into his mouth. "My compliments to the chef."

My stomach turned, but Birdie kept her cool and class. She flat out ignored him.

"Come now, girls. If everyone is finished, let's move this party into the library. It's time for games and dessert."

CHAPTER EIGHT

I was so disgusted by Birdie's nephew, I didn't think I'd want dessert, but, silly me, that was before I saw what Chef Perry had cooked up.

The library had completely transformed from day to night. The fire had been stoked. The tree, lit. Aviation gear—caps, scarves, goggles—adorned the branches. A giant, glistening propeller topped the tree instead of the usual star. And branches of fresh pine entwined with ribbons and lights spruced up the mantel. My toes tingled with excitement.

"I've never seen the library look so enchanting. It's like a fairy tale," Birdie said. She then flitted about the room like a butterfly. She buried her nose in the evergreen, made a fuss over the twin candelabras, complimented every poinsettia, and turned the gorgeous tree ever so slightly so its "best side faced out." I half expected her to pinch its sweet cheeks and straighten its tie. Standing back, she sighed happily.

Meanwhile, Collin had seated himself in the corner and cracked open a huge book, *Much Ado about Stuffing: Taxidermy for Everyone*. A red fox graced the cover, dressed in a bow tie and posed in a cushy chair. I adored foxes as much as I despised rats, which got me to wondering how exactly Collin acquired his specimens. I didn't approve of hunting animals for sport, except for sewer rats. Their ancestors gave us the bubonic plague, and they've now evolved enough to swim up toilet bowls. How's that for a nightmare? Speaking of nightmares, Collin probably missed something important—say, organizing the carcasses in his freezer—to be here. And thanks to the storm, he was most likely stuck for the night in a drafty old house with the six of us. *Gulp*. I turned my three-by-three over in my pocket. Maybe I should say hello, to get on his good side.

But before I could introduce myself, the room erupted into gasps and applause.

Edna drew back the drapes to the reading room to reveal a glossy buffet loaded with sweets and the largest, most elaborate gingerbread house I'd ever seen.

We swarmed the table like flies.

I pushed past the antique piano and the portrait of Amelia's grandmother with her too-tight bun for a closer look at the spread. Chef Perry was a magician. This confectionary feat, with its two stories, pitched roof, curved windows, clapboard siding, and wide front porch, put my graham-cracker-and-gumdrop houses to shame. A degree in rocket science wasn't required to see this was the Amelia Earhart Birthplace Museum in gingerbread form. Chef Perry nailed every detail, down to the piped-on balcony.

It was so beautiful I wanted to touch it, but I knew better. One tiny bump could collapse the whole structure.

"Look at the deliciousness," Thea mumbled. "I wonder how many hours he spent decorating."

"Too many. Do you think it's all edible?" asked Wren.

I shook my head. "Only a monster would eat that. It's too pretty!"

Wren rolled her eyes. "You'd never survive a zombie apocalypse."

Thankfully, we didn't have to find out. Chef Perry was wheeling in a hot cocoa bar as we spoke. It held six mini cheesecakes and a tiny chalkboard sign:

ENJOY A CUP OF COCOA LIKE AMELIA!
Amelia sipped hot cocoa on this history-making flight.
What: First ever solo flight across the Atlantic (2,408 miles)
When: January 11, 1935
Where: From Honolulu, HI, to Oakland, CA

Jars filled with mini marshmallows, cinnamon sticks, caramel bits, sprinkles, and classic peppermint candy canes flooded the cart. And at the far end, fresh whipped cream billowed like a cloud from a big crystal bowl. Heaven on earth.

I made my mug of hot chocolate (with extra sprinkles, of course) and dolloped the whipped cream on both my cocoa and cheesecake, because why not? No grown-ups were here to tell me no. Then I carefully situated myself on the plush couch between Thea and Nathalie, all of us juggling our fancy fare.

"Amelia didn't like coffee or tea, so she drank hot chocolate to stay awake," Thea said, watching steam rise from her cup.

"I support that," Nathalie said. She slipped a crumble of cheesecake crust into her pocket, and I broke out in a cold sweat. Rosie Stancer could crawl out at any moment and give us all cardiac arrests. And I'd be the one who would spill hot cocoa all over Amelia Earhart's grandmother's Victorian sofa. Which was probably as old as Queen Victoria herself.

Sandwiched on the other couch, the sisters and Cassie swapped stories of honest-to-goodness astronauts they'd met. I licked whipped cream from my lip and tried to think if I'd ever met anyone really and truly famous. I once met the governor at a state cubing competition, but I'm not sure she counted. Now, Mom? Mom knew some famous pilots. She'd bunked with her friend Java, one of the first female fighter pilots, a Bronze Star recipient, and sender of holiday cards signed *Love, J*. She'd had coffee with Mélanie Astles, Red Bull's only female pilot, and Patty Wagstaff, the first woman to win the US National Aerobatic Championships. You know, the ones who do death-defying stunts at two thousand feet up when most of us would panic and pee our pants.

Then I looked at Birdie. She exuded confidence in her turtleneck and gigantic square glasses. She sipped her cocoa and settled happily into the wingback chair cozied up to the fireplace. Her cane rested against her leg, and she looked so at ease I thought she should throw elegant parties every night.

Electra moseyed over and curled up near her feet.

"Achoo!" Robin sneezed, and somehow didn't spill a drop of her drink.

I took a bite of my cheesecake—savoring the buttery almond crust—and waited for . . . what? I wasn't sure, exactly.

As if she could read my mind, Birdie set her cocoa down and cleared her throat. "Cassie, would you please fetch the packages underneath the tree? And do be careful of the ornaments."

I nudged Nathalie and strained my neck to see around the girls lined up on the sofa.

Neither of us had even noticed the gifts. Cassie hadn't either, as she let out a surprised "Oh!"

She held up a brown paper package tied with a wide red ribbon. Birdie nodded. "One for everyone, please."

I was positively giddy as Cassie played Santa's elf, delivering a wrapped present to each of us. This whole night seemed magical, if not too good to be true. Cozy snowflakes.

Scrumptious food. A crackling fire. And now, beautifully wrapped gifts. I gave mine a little shake. Whatever it was rustled inside. It felt mysterious and exciting.

"These gifts are from the Ninety-Nines. Go ahead, open them," Birdie encouraged.

I glanced about the room and tugged on the shiny ribbon.

"Oh, cool," Thea said, lifting the lid to her box.

I slipped my fingernail underneath the tape, rushing to see what was inside.

Layers of tissue paper crinkled as I pushed them aside to reveal . . . a leather flight cap. My own vintage flight cap, just like Amelia's. Only mine was stamped with the initials *A.A.* on the inside for me, Amelia Ashford. But that wasn't all. There were also flight goggles and a small cardboard box stamped with the Ninety-Nines' logo—two square nines interlocked—reflected in silver foil.

I opened the box and gasped. Inside was a card embossed with airplane wings. Punched through the center was a shiny new pin with an airplane and the number six.

"Oh my goodness," said Robin. "I love it."

"It's amazing!" said Thea, wearing her new goggles on her face and her original pair on top of her head. "What is it, exactly?"

Birdie grinned. "I'm so glad you approve. The Ninety-Nines designed these limited-edition pins just for you."

"Really?" I said. "Thank you."

Birdie smiled. "You are welcome. As are all of you, the Amelia Six."

The hair on my arms stood up. "The Amelia Six, huh? I like that."

"Me too," said Nathalie.

"Cool," said Wren, having fastened her pin to her shirt.

"I thought of handing out the goggles before dinner, only you wouldn't have been able to see what you were eating." Birdie chuckled.

"You can say that again." Wren slipped her goggles on and stuck out her tongue.

Birdie smiled. "If it's all right with you, I would like a group photo by the desserts to send to the members. Edna, would you mind?"

Edna took a camera down from the mantel. I hurriedly put on my flight cap and positioned the goggles across my forehead like everyone else had done. Giggling, we gathered around Birdie.

"Say 'wings'!" chirped Edna.

"Wings!" we shouted.

The flash went off, and white light blinded me. *Oops.* Someone stepped backward into me. Electra yowled.

My arms flew out as I tried to maintain my balance, but I felt myself falling in slow motion. Right into the gingerbread house.

CHAPTER NINE

Nooo.

Horrified gasps surrounded me as my elbow crashed onto the table. In one swift motion, I took out the peppermint lamppost, scraped snow off the sugary walk, and demolished the front porch. It was made of pretzels. But no sooner had I begun to panic than everyone else laughed with relief.

The house itself was fine. Leaning, but standing.

"That was a close one, kid," Perry said. "Are you okay?"

Horrified, I stood and looked from him to Birdie. "I'm fine. I'm so sorry. I don't know what happened. I lost my balance and—"

Birdie waved her arm and shushed me. "It was an accident. Accidents happen. They're part of living. This can all be fixed."

"Easily." Perry winked and started for the kitchen. "I'll get more sugar."

Still, my cheeks burned hot. I was a clumsy idiot.

Cassie gave me a smile. "At least Edna snapped the picture first."

"I bet it's a good one too." Robin turned to Wren. "Let's ask for permission to post it online."

"Yum. Rosie loves pretzels," Nathalie said, and reached for one of the broken bits.

Thea brushed her hand away. "Uh-uh." She pulled a small tube from her pocket. "Watch this."

Carefully, Thea unscrewed the cap and dabbed dots of glue onto the pretzels. In quiet concentration, she pieced the porch together like some kind of wizard. Her time spent building miniatures with her family had paid off. Thea waited a few more seconds, long enough for the glue to dry, then repaired the lamppost. "Good as new." She straightened her back and smiled.

"Hooray," Nathalie said, clapping. "But why do you have superglue?"

Thea shrugged. "In case something needs fixing."

Perry returned and spread sugar over the miniature yard—it really did look like snow. "You know, when I was your age, I had a Rubik's Cube," he said.

Oh brother, here we go.

"Yeah?" I steeled myself for what always came next. The

story of how they solved it by removing all the stickers.

"Yeah. And most of my friends cheated by taking off the stickers, but I wasn't like them."

Huh.

Perry added a dusting of sugar to the porch to hide the new cracks. "I got to where I could actually solve it. Not superfast, mind you. But I figured it out on my own."

"Wow," I said. "That's great. You're welcome to try mine." I held out my cube.

Perry laughed. "I don't even know if I remember how! Let me get the kitchen cleaned first."

I smiled. "You're on."

Birdie fished a stack of bright envelopes from her chair and whistled shrilly. Everyone stopped and stared.

Even Collin quit studying to see what the newest fuss was about.

"Millie, will you please pass these out?" asked Birdie.

"Sure." I set my goggles on the table. This was a chance to redeem myself.

Each envelope was sealed and bore a name across the front in swirling script.

AMELIA ASHFORD stretched across the red envelope. Red like Amelia's plane. Amelia, the name Mom had given me. Though Dad preferred Millie, as it was closer to Miles. I shuffled through the stack, delivering each letter.

"Well, don't just sit there. Open them!" Birdie said.

I slipped my finger underneath the flap and pulled out a

piece of folded paper. It appeared to be a list of riddles. Eight riddles, to be exact, and at the top right corner of the page, the number three was circled in red. I glanced at Nathalie. She shrugged.

Wren and Robin compared their papers while Thea read silently to herself, her lips moving with the words.

"What do you make of it?" Birdie drummed her skinny fingers on her armrest.

I studied the list:

1. Find and name Amelia's favorite childhood toy. You might say it's as stubborn as a mule.

2. Before Amelia ever wore a flight cap, she donned *this* cap at the start of WWI.

3. Amelia flew in the United States' first Women's Air Derby in 1929. Find her trophy to see where she placed.

4. Amelia famously flew with this First Lady, whom she considered a good friend.

5. He proposed six times before she said yes.

6. Name the Pacific island that was Amelia's next destination when she disappeared.

7. An early adopter, Amelia used *this* method of transportation to zip around airports at a whopping fifteen mph.

8. You may wear these while swimming, but Amelia wore them on her most heroic flight because they fit her "unconventional _____" best. Must list year.

I smirked and touched the tip of my own nose. Obviously, I knew the answer to the last one, though I couldn't let on that I did.

"This looks like a scavenger hunt," I said.

"Or test," Cassie offered.

"Bingo!" Birdie said with a smile. "That's exactly what it is. A scavenger hunt. To put your Amelia facts to the test. Though no grades will be given at the end. Only prizes."

"Awesome." Wren chugged her cocoa and wiped her chocolate mustache off with the back of her hand. "Let's go."

"Wait. Can we use our devices?" Thea asked.

Birdie smiled and pointed to a basket by her feet. "Afraid not, Thea. All phones and electronics will need to be deposited in this basket, which I will lock up for safekeeping. This ensures everyone plays fair and square."

"But we promised our viewers," Wren protested.

"I trust you'll remember enough to write up a stellar post,

Wren. And you may take all the photos you want once the game is over."

Wren made a face, but Robin mouthed, *It's fine.* They added their phones. As did Cassie (her case looked fancy) and Thea and Nathalie. Then it was my turn.

My fingers closed around the smooth metal, still warm from being in my pocket. My chest grew tight. Anxiety snaked its way up from my stomach and wrapped its cool claws around my heart. I bit my lip.

Sure, the screen was broken, but my phone worked. It was my one direct line to Dad. He'd bought it for me in case there was another emergency. But there would be no emergencies, not tonight. My phone would be locked up for only a couple of hours. As long as one silly game. Still, I found it hard to let go.

Edna shook the basket under my nose, and I dropped my phone inside.

CHAPTER TEN

Edna spun on her heel, marched to the bookcase, and shoved our phones inside. I really did not like that woman. Not one bit.

"Thank you, Edna," Birdie said, locking the cabinet door. "Now, girls, pay attention. Everything you need to complete the scavenger hunt can be found in the house itself. And here's the exciting part. There is a *prize*." Birdie clapped her hands in enthusiasm.

"This keeps getting better." Wren cracked her knuckles.

"Shhh," Cassie said.

Birdie kept on. "Everyone's list of items is the same; however, the number circled at the top matches you to your teammate."

Teams? My heart sank. I worked best alone. But if I

had to be on a team, I hoped I was on Thea's. Or maybe Nathalie's . . . if Rosie stayed hidden.

"Who has number one?" Birdie asked.

Nathalie and Robin raised their hands.

"Number two?"

"Me," Cassie said.

"And me," Thea repeated with a sigh.

"Great," said Wren. "That leaves me and the puzzle queen."

I held up my lucky cube and smiled at Wren. "That's me!" I tried to sound excited, but I could tell Wren was still ticked her phone was locked up. That made two of us.

"What's the prize?" Cassie asked.

Birdie's smile stretched a mile wide. "The team that finds all or a majority of the items first *and* brings their sheet, answered correctly, back to me gets to . . ."

She clasped her hands underneath her chin and drew in a big breath. "Gets to spend the night in Amelia's own bedroom! With cookies and milk at midnight in their new souvenir mugs."

Cassie turned to Thea. "We're so going to win."

And immediately something stirred inside my chest. I looked at my list and at Wren. And I knew she was thinking what I was. We had to win. She needed to win for her viewers. I needed to win for my mom. Maybe then we'd have something to talk about the next time she called.

I checked the grandfather clock. "When do we start?"

Birdie held out a bouquet of sharpened pencils. "How about now?"

Wren and I raced out of the library and across the foyer into the old men's parlor on the north side of the house. One dim lamp burned in the corner, and a radiator hissed somewhere in the dark. I wanted to study the pictures on the walls, but we had to discuss our strategy. That, and I had no flashlight.

"Okay. Listen, I know the last one. It's 'nose.' She had an unconventional nose."

"You're kidding, right?"

"No," I said, and quickly spilled my earlier discovery. "I thought I'd found another bedroom, only it was some weird room with jewelry and costumed mannequins and luggage!" I waved the scavenger list.

Wren punched me in the arm. "Shh! You've got to keep your voice down."

I nodded. My fingers shook with excitement. Blood whooshed through my ears. "And her goggles. Her goggles were there. I saw them!"

Feet pounded up the stairs. I peered through a tiny arched window (later I learned it was an old phone shelf) to catch a glimpse of Thea's boots disappearing upstairs, which meant Cassie was ahead of her. We had to act fast.

"Are you sure?" Wren ran a hand through her hair.

I nodded.

"Do you remember the year?"

"No." I shook my head and took a step back, afraid she'd smack my arm again.

"We'll get it later," Wren huffed, and scrawled the word "nose" in the blank on number eight. "Okay. Birdie said earlier that Amelia's engagement portrait was in here."

We turned around, and voilà!

The portrait was impossible to miss, even in the dim light. The painting's thick gold frame contrasted beautifully against the parlor's wine-and-gray wallpaper. And Amelia, leaning slightly against her soon-to-be husband, looked relaxed but determined. She wore a flowy cream blouse, a smart green jacket with four brass buttons, and a Mona Lisa smile. Her fiancé looked serious in a dark suit, red tie, and rimless glasses. His brown hair had a Superman-like wave.

"I have a theory she never wanted to marry," Wren said.

Amelia stared straight ahead with an almost amused expression.

"The clue said he proposed six times. But who's he?" I squinted to read the sign.

Wren skimmed the plaque. "George Palmer Putnam. Or, as I call him, the answer to riddle number five. Publisher, author, explorer, and, most notably, Amelia's husband and business manager. Look at their marriage certificate. . . . Amelia kept her own name for flying, like a boss."

I leaned forward for a better look at a framed copy of their marriage license, but Wren was already pulling me through a swinging door into the old butler's pantry. Save for a trough-sized sink and a tall wooden cupboard, the space now resembled a strategic mission headquarters more than a food-prep space. Maps and posters tracking Amelia's disappearance covered the walls. And the white enameled sink held watered houseplants, not produce waiting to be scrubbed. A small table sat in one corner by the lace-draped window, and I could almost imagine servants or Amelia and her sister, Muriel, enjoying a meal.

"We have to find the name of the island. You take that wall, and I'll check this one."

"Got it." I studied the world map in front of me. A long red string, tacked down with metal pushpins, dipped and bobbed across the United States from Oakland to Miami, then stretched into South America and across the Atlantic to Africa, India, and Thailand.

"Wren. I think I found it." My heart sped up as my finger traced the length of red thread. "Oakland, California. May twenty-first, 1937. Then Burbank, Tucson, New Orleans. Miami on June first. Each pin represents a stopover city and date."

"Did you say Miami? Her plane was last serviced in

Miami." Excited, Wren whacked my upper arm. "So, if we keep following . . ."

Ow. I rubbed the sore spot but smiled. "If we keep following the line into the Pacific . . ."

Wren waved me to her side. "Check out this paragraph. Monsoons and airplane maintenance delayed her departure from Indonesia on June twenty-seventh. Then two days later, in Darwin, Australia, this note says she 'possibly *mailed her parachutes home.*'"

"What?" Incredulous, I doubled-checked the map. Bingo: It put her in Australia on the twenty-ninth. "I guess parachutes don't do much good when you're only over water. Look here—the map shows she left Lae, New Guinea, next on July second. Then the string runs out." I tapped my fingernail on a tiny island in the Pacific. "This red dot must mark their final destination! Wren, we're one step closer to spending the night in Amelia Earhart's room!"

CHAPTER ELEVEN

"Shhh, Sherlock." Wren smoothed an old article tacked next to the map. "I'm reading."

I jammed my hands into my pockets. This game was as nerve-racking as standardized tests. Only the end goal was greater, and even though we had newly sharpened number 2s, we had no calculator or practice test. We had to win this. Had. To.

"Whoa," Wren mumbled, still reading. "Howland Island. That's the island, all right. Amelia and her navigator took off from Lae at ten a.m. local time, headed for Howland, and were never seen again. They must have run out of fuel and crashed into the sea."

"Or maybe they landed somewhere else and starved," I guessed.

Wren stared at the map. "No one knows. Some think she could have even been a spy. But Howland Island's it."

I scanned the scavenger hunt list and wrote "Howland" next to number six.

"I heard she shipped back a bracelet made from an elephant hoof. It was her good luck charm. But she mailed it to her husband, this Mr. Putnam, the day before she disappeared. Eerie, huh?" I shuddered.

Wren nodded. "Tempting fate. But Lae to Howland would have been their longest flight. They needed to make the plane as light as possible to preserve fuel. But it does make you wonder if she could have survived had she kept more gear on board."

"Like her precious freckle cream?" Cassie asked, waltzing into the room.

"Oh," Wren griped, "like you know better."

Cassie crossed her arms. "Then why'd she keep the cream but not her Morse code manual? Sounds like a huge mistake to me. Almost as big as Birdie sending those historic goggles to the Smithsonian. Everyone knows they belong at Purdue."

"*Everyone* doesn't, or the goggles would be going there," Wren said with a laugh.

Cassie squared her shoulders. "Amelia taught at Purdue! She lived on campus, ate with students, and was loved by everyone. Purdue bought her last plane, for crying out loud."

"Yeah, but I'm sure Birdie and the Ninety-Nines discussed—"

"Let it go, Wren," I said, waving the scavenger list. "We're losing valuable time."

"Who's losing?" Thea asked as she clomped across the thin carpet to her partner. The scavenger list was in her hand, and she looked a bit miserable as she swiped her hair out of her eyes.

"No one," I replied. "This is harder than it looks."

Thea grunted. "You got that right. Our invitations should have come with a warning for us to brush up on Amelia trivia. Though I did know the one about Eleanor Roosevelt."

Cassie huffed. "Everyone knows that story, Thea. It's not every day the First Lady ditches a dinner at the White House to go flying with a famous aviatrix."

I glanced at my list and made a little mark next to number four.

Wren saw my pencil moving. "Well. Maybe not *everyone*."

My cheeks burned.

"Aww. Don't worry, Millie. They were back in time for dessert." Thea laughed.

"True." Wren sighed. "Of course, the press was more interested in their fancy dresses than the flight itself."

Thea rolled her eyes. "Of course."

"So, Eleanor Roosevelt. Got it," I said, scribbling in the answer. Anything to move on to the next question. Maybe I didn't know every last detail there was to know about Amelia Earhart, but I knew this much: I was spending the night in that room. Then I was going to find my mother and tell her all about it. My toes tingled just thinking about how happy she'd be.

I was busy skimming the next clue when Chef Perry loped into the room like a Saint Bernard. A dish towel hung from his shoulder, and his arms were loaded with dried pots and pans.

"Sorry to eavesdrop, but cookware doesn't store itself." He opened a cabinet. "Did you see the photo of Amelia and Eleanor at the White House dinner? Simply stunning! There's a copy of the menu around here somewhere."

Cassie jabbed her thumb toward me and Wren. "*We* were just discussing that."

Wren stuck out her chin.

"Aha. Friendly competition," Perry said with a smile. "In the restaurant world, we call that 'cutthroat kitchen.'" A thin line of sweat dotted his upper lip, and his sleeves were pushed up above his elbows. His tattoo was most definitely an airplane. A biplane, to be exact, with the letters *G-EBOV* on the body in all caps.

"Do you fly?" I asked, feeling a bit nosy.

Perry laughed and shook his head. "Oh no. I'm just a big Amelia fan."

"Perry!" Collin hollered from the breezeway. "Do you have any milk?"

Perry's shoulders slumped. "Excuse me. I'd better hurry."

"Of course," I said, jumping out of his way.

"We were leaving anyway," Wren added as she dragged me along through the chilly breezeway into the gift shop.

"I thought we'd never get out of there!" I whispered, stopping in front of the shop's glorious collection of rare Amelia memorabilia for sale.

"Quick. There's no time to shop. We have to beat them to the nurse's cap and goggles."

"Nurse's cap?" I repeated, browsing the beautiful mahogany-and-glass cabinet flanked by crowded, if not dusty, bookshelves. Edna wasn't that great a housekeeper.

"Yes." Wren took the list from me. "Have you never read a biography of Amelia? She was a nurse's aide for the Red Cross during World War I. The second answer is 'a nurse's hat.'"

"Like this one?" I pointed to a white cap on the top shelf.

"Well done, Sherlock." Wren smiled.

"And look, down below is answer number three. The 1929 Women's National Air Derby," I added.

Wren cupped her hands around her eyes and peered into the cabinet at a blown-up, grainy photograph of a group of female pilots. They formed a line behind a row of glistening trophies of varying heights, some waist high. The picture's caption identified Amelia (positioned just right of center) as the third-place winner. The pilot standing on the far left in a white-striped tee took first place. I squinted to read her name: Louise M. Thaden.

Louise must have been an amazing aviator to beat Amelia.

"Good. Now, stop cubing and follow me."

"Sorry." I winced, unaware that I'd pulled my Rubik's Cube out. I made three quick turns and stuffed the puzzle back into my pocket. When I looked up, Wren was moving the display case away from the wall.

Correction—the display case was swinging out on its own. The hairs on my arms stood up. If this house turned out to be haunted or, worse, run by a supernatural species of rats . . . I was out.

"Wren?" I gulped. "What is going on?"

"Shh!" she whispered. "Follow me."

And she disappeared into the dark.

CHAPTER TWELVE

I could have cursed Birdie for pairing me with Wren. Wren was bold, brave, and the exact opposite of me. Wren had cool pink hair and silver moon boots. I had sweaty palms and an intense fear of rodents, mold, natural disasters, and calamities in general. It's not that I thought the world was out to get me, but I couldn't be too careful.

"We don't have all day, Ashford."

The case began sliding slowly back into place. Wren waved at me to hurry as another team, maybe Nathalie and Robin, raced down the hallway.

Drat.

I had no choice but to follow Wren. We were partners. Partners who wanted to win. I slipped into the darkness, and the door sealed me inside like a tomb.

I squeezed my eyes shut.

Breathe, Millie.

Breathe.

Wren tugged at a chain dangling from the ceiling, and warm light flooded the musty space. I sucked air into my lungs. We hadn't stumbled upon another pantry or storage closet, though there were ancient cans of tomato juice stacked along the wall. What we'd found was the landing to a secret staircase.

"Whoa." I brushed a cobweb out of my hair.

"Told you," Wren whispered. "Let's go."

"No way. Not until you tell me how you knew this was here."

Wren smirked. "I didn't. It was a lucky hunch."

I crossed my arms.

"Okay, the depth of the shelves seemed off, so I tried to move that dusty bust of Judge Otis, and the whole thing swung open. I'm being serious. Think about it: a Civil War–era home built on a bluff, next to a rail line. They could have been part of the Underground Railroad. Lots of those homes had safe rooms or secret passages. Plus, Judge Otis was the bank president, remember?"

"Oh my gosh, Wren. You're right."

She smirked. "I try. Keep your voice down and step carefully. These boards are old." Wren tried out the first step, and then the second. So far, so good.

"Wait!" I whispered. Wren turned around.

"Where does this lead?"

Wren shrugged. "Up?"

Somehow that didn't make me feel any better.

We crept up fourteen stairs. At the top there was a solid wooden door. It looked like any other antique oak door, one that would lead to a bedroom or a closet. Of course, we had no idea where this one led. Or what was waiting on the other side.

Wren put one hand on the knob. With the other, she motioned for me to turn out the light. I tugged on the chain, and midnight engulfed us. The only sound was my own beating heart. I counted . . . one Mississippi.

Two Mississippi.

Three Mississippi.

Wren cracked the door open.

She peered into the wide hallway upstairs, relieved to see we were obscured by the potted palm. The coast was clear.

But we had to move fast.

Quickly, I slipped out into the empty hallway. Wren followed, pushing the door closed.

I tucked my hair behind my ears and, to quiet my racing thoughts, pulled out the list to make it look like we were casually strolling. I skimmed the piece of paper and looked back at the potted plant. No one would know a door was there unless she knew to look for it. There was no knob on the outside, only a small metal latch that blended into the gold wallpaper.

"That room. That's where we go next." I pointed to the doorway across the hall.

"The goggles?" asked Wren, her eyebrows raised.

"Yeah." I nodded and led the way.

But as soon as I reached the door, Robin rushed out. She looked shaky and pale, like she'd seen Amelia's ghost.

Wren grabbed her sister by the arm. "Robin, are you okay? What's wrong?"

"The goggles," she whispered. "The goggles are gone."

CHAPTER THIRTEEN

"Gone? What do you mean, 'gone'?" asked Wren.

Robin's hands trembled in front of her mouth. "Someone stole them," she whispered. "*Stole* them."

Wren looked at me, and I shook my head, confused. "Impossible. They were just there."

Wren bowled by me. "Come on, Ashford. She'll need a witness."

For the second time this evening, against my better judgment, I followed Wren. The mannequin room looked exactly the same. Creepy. Like a wax museum. At first glance, nothing seemed amiss. But something was, all right—the main attraction. Amelia Earhart's goggles no longer sat on a carpet of red velvet inside a glass display case. The goggles didn't appear to be anywhere. And the only witnesses were posed plastic figures who couldn't speak.

Wren put her hand up. "Hold on. Where's Nathalie?"

"Right here."

Nathalie emerged from behind the display case. "I don't see any evidence of tampering."

"You didn't touch it, did you?" I whispered. "If they're truly stolen, the police will dust for fingerprints."

"The police," Wren said with a huff. "If they can even get here in this blizzard."

Robin brushed a strand of hair from her face. "Guys, what if this is a piece of the scavenger hunt?"

Nathalie's eyes lit up. "Ooh, you mean the goggles could be a part of the game."

"I hope you're right," I said. "I'd feel better if this was a way for us to level up."

"Like we're supposed to find Amelia Earhart's actual flight goggles," Wren scoffed.

"What? Is that so unbelievable?" Robin asked.

"They wouldn't trust us with such an important piece of history, you goof." Wren walked around the case, observing every angle.

"It'd be a really weird twist," I agreed. "Look! The thief dropped the Fernstrom letter," I said, picking it up off the floor.

"Fernstrom?" Robin asked.

"Oh. He found her goggles the last time they disappeared. See?"

Robin turned toward me. "You mean they've gone missing before?"

"Apparently." I gave her the typed page.

Nathalie pulled Rosie out of her pocket and gave her a crumb of cheesecake. "Okay, this is creeping me out. We should tell Birdie."

Wren crouched in front of the mannequin wearing a vintage flight suit. "Or we try to find the goggles ourselves first."

"You can't be serious." I crossed my arms.

"Oh, she's serious, all right." Robin sighed.

"Ow." Wren hopped up and inspected her hand.

"Are you okay?" I asked.

"Yeah," she said. "There's something sharp . . ." She bent down and picked up a gold fleck from the floor.

"What is it?" asked Nathalie.

Wren shrugged. "Looks like an earring."

"May I see?" I turned the piece over to catch the light. "Aww. It's a tiny gold bird, covered in crystals. Wren's palm probably came down on its pointy wings."

"Pointy, sharp wings," she corrected.

"I bet Birdie has a lost and found," said Robin.

"Good idea." I tucked the earring into my front pocket for safekeeping. "Meanwhile, what's next?"

"We tell Birdie about the missing goggles," Nathalie stated, cradling her pet. "Right, Rosie?"

Wren shook her head. "No. First we search Amelia's room."

"But it's off-limits," I said. "We'll jeopardize our chance at the prize."

"Not if we find them first. The more I think on it, Robin's got to be right. It's part of the game! Rules were made to be broken. They're testing us." Wren's face flushed with excitement.

Uneasiness hit my stomach like too many doughnuts. I pulled the cube from my pocket. Spinning its sides helped settle my anxious brain. "I don't know . . ."

Wren tapped her foot. "Quit stalling. WWAD. *What Would Amelia Do?* Amelia would look."

Nathalie nodded. "She was a total risk taker."

"She was more than that. She was a nonconformist. A fearless feminist," added Robin. "I should write a poem."

"Not now, Robin." Wren turned and plucked my cube from my hands. "Brava, Millie! You solved it. Let's go."

I looked at my cube. The yellow side glared at me. Yellow, the color of Amelia's first airplane, a used biplane she bought on her twenty-fifth birthday after working a dozen odd jobs. She called it "the Canary."

I laughed even though part of me wanted to cry. Yellow typically meant "caution," but for Amelia it meant "fly."

"What's so funny?" asked Robin.

"Nothing," I said. "Let's go."

We reached the bedroom, and the four of us stopped to gawk. From the roped-off doorway, anyone could see that the Earhart sisters' room was something special. Buttery yellow paper with watercolor wildflowers wrapped around the walls, from the wooden floorboards to the high ceiling. Dark beams outlined the windows and made up the tall closet door. An iron bed painted the exact shade of vanilla ice cream was shoved against the wall to the left and piled high with dreamy pastel quilting. It looked to be the perfect spot for napping or building blanket forts. I imagined Amelia, with a plate of cookies, reading and daydreaming. Across the room, an antique dresser held a huge mirror and porcelain pitcher for washing. And in the corner, next to the wide window with a view of the river, stood a dress form fitted with a frock Amelia, according to the sign on the wall, had designed herself. The room was straight out of a storybook.

Perfect and untouched.

"No one's set foot in here." Robin pointed to the rope lashed across the doorway.

"Not true," said Wren. "Look at the floor."

The unmistakable outline of a footprint was faintly evident in the dust on the floorboard. Which caused me to wonder if Edna had even swept this room ahead of our arrival. Maybe it was off-limits to her, too. Or maybe she had missed a spot. Or maybe this was all part of the game. Whichever way, it was something.

"Everything looks perfectly staged," I whispered. "Not a

pillow or drawer is out of place. If someone did move the flight goggles here, they did so carefully."

"Well, the print is pointing toward the closet," Nathalie said. "And it looks big. Like a man's footprint, or at least a snow boot."

"Maybe it's Santa's," I joked.

Wren rolled her eyes. "Very funny. This house has three chimneys, and none are in here."

"Fine. I like Nathalie's suggestion," I said. "Someone moved something into storage. The print is right by the closet door."

"Then I nominate you to check it out."

My heart stopped. "Me? No."

Wren untied the rope stretching across the doorway and waited two full seconds before giving me a shove. "Rules were meant to be broken, right? You're not doing this for us, but for humanity. Those goggles are a historic artifact and need to be shared with the world."

"Are you sure we shouldn't just tell Birdie?" I winced. "She wouldn't have stashed a scavenger hunt item in a room that was strictly forbidden."

"It's not forbidden. The room is clearly open to the scavenger hunt winners, which we will be as soon as you get a move on. Now, go! Or Thea and Cassie will win the whole thing."

I stepped gingerly across the floor. My heart rate picked

up. My eye twitched. How had I gotten myself into this mess? I was the straight-as-an-arrow, follow-the-rules type of good girl. I did not trespass. Which was entering a person's private property without their permission, an illegal activity, and precisely what I was doing right now.

"Just one more step, and you've got it," Wren whispered loud enough to wake the dead. "That's it. Now reach out your hand and turn the knob."

The knob to Amelia's closet was oval and black and had a fancy-pants lock plate. I hesitated to grip the cool metal. My fingers shook, so I thought WWAD, and *click*—

The door swung open.

"Well?" Nathalie asked.

I took a deep breath and peered inside.

"Christmas decorations."

Wren's face fell. "That's it?" She wanted to spend the night in Amelia's room as much as I did.

I stepped into the dark. Pine needles prickled my skin. A Christmas tree blocked my path. Slowly, my eyes adjusted to the shadows, and I shifted items on the shelves: Wreaths. Ribbon. A box of old ornaments. But no goggles.

"Promise." I pushed aside the artificial spruce so they could see for themselves.

And that's when a hand grabbed my arm.

CHAPTER FOURTEEN

Of course, I screamed.

I screamed like no one had screamed in the history of screaming. I knew this had been a horrible idea. Snooping in Amelia Earhart's closet, which was off-limits, and quite possibly haunted. But Wren and the other girls had insisted. So, I went along with them instead of resisting, which is what I should have done, and now a meaty paw had a death grip on my wrist.

"Would you hush? I'm not going to hurt you. I was trying to not spook you."

My voice climbed two octaves. "By hiding in the closet? And grabbing my arm?"

Collin released his grip. "I wasn't hiding. I was checking traps. See?" He held up a catch-and-release mousetrap.

Nathalie paled and put a protective hand over her pocket.

"I didn't want you to step on it," Collin said.

"Thank you," I squeaked. "Is there a, uh, specimen inside?"

"Nah, this trap's as empty as a tomb."

Wren, unafraid of vermin, dead or alive, marched closer. She put her nose right next to the plastic box of doom and sniffed.

"Smells like sweaty socks, not death. He's telling the truth."

"Honest truth." Collin ran his hand through his wavy hair. "Aunt Birdie's been hearing rustlings in the walls at night, and Perry said he spotted rodent droppings in the kitchen. Since Electra's older and not as great of a mouser, my aunt asked me to place some traps. I thought I'd check this one before you spent the night in here."

Wren stepped back and crossed her arms. "Then why'd you close the door?"

Collin shook his head. "I didn't. It swung shut on me, I swear."

"Huh." Wren sat on the edge of the bed. "You haven't checked traps in any other room?"

Collin shook his head. "This was the first one." His hands were open, out of his pockets, and he looked us straight in the eyes. His body language said he was telling the truth, but my instincts didn't trust him. There was something shifty about the way he carried himself, down to his boots and his black-and-gold socks.

"So, if you didn't enter the mannequin room, then who did?"

"That's the question of the hour, isn't it?" a voice trilled behind us.

I whirled around to find Birdie standing in the hallway alongside Edna, Thea, Cassie, and Chef Perry, armed with a small frying pan.

Edna's cheeks flushed with excitement or anger. It was hard to tell with her. She looked perpetually cross. Cassie's face looked expressionless, if not calculating, while Thea's eyes were filled with questions. And Birdie's stance, with her skinny shoulders thrust back, her red lips pressed together, and her cool eyes ablaze, looked charged. She was on fire— figuratively speaking, of course. There was no real fire.

Yet.

"What. Is. Going. On?" Birdie punctuated each word by tapping her cane against the floor. "I want facts. No opinions."

Oh boy. I looked at Thea with her goggles propped on top of her head. She winced. How could one night turn so wrong?

"Did I miss my invitation to a silent retreat? Not everyone at once, now." Birdie's voice was stern. "Collin, as the responsible adult in the room, let's start with you."

I wanted to dive underneath Amelia's bed and stay there until this brouhaha was over.

Collin's chest puffed out, and he grew defensive. "I was

checking the traps in the closet like we discussed, Aunt Birdie, and these girls snuck into the room. They completely ignored the fact that this room is closed. Anyway, one of them got spooked and screamed. End of story."

I stared at the floor, my cheeks hot.

"Ha," Wren blurted. "We wouldn't have even entered, but Amelia's goggles are *gone*."

Birdie drew a sharp breath. "I knew it," she whispered, placing her hand over her heart and looking pained.

"Are you okay, Birdie?" I asked, mentally reviewing the signs and symptoms of heart attacks in females: chest pressure, extreme fatigue and nausea, shortness of breath, pain in jaw or arms . . .

Birdie waved me aside.

"Wren," she said, and walked over so that she was nose to nose with the Winters sister. "This is no time for joking. Are you sure?"

Wren gulped and nodded. "You mean it's not part of the game?"

Behind me, Cassie huffed, clearly annoyed by our stupidity. Like it was our fault the museum's most famous possession had disappeared.

"It's true," Robin spoke a decibel or two above a whisper. "The case is empty."

Birdie thumped her cane against the floor again. "I've lived in this house for over thirty years without an ounce of trouble, and now this happens." Her voice broke. "And right before the Smithsonian arrives."

Collin threw up his hands. "I told you to donate them to the school. How many times did I say you don't have the security and surveillance of a big institution?"

"Not helpful, Collin." Perry placed his hand on Birdie's shoulder. "We'll find whoever did this, Birdie. Don't you worry."

"Justice would be nice, of course. But all I really care about is the goggles themselves. I need them to be safe and sound." She pointed her cane at Wren. "Show me exactly what you found."

Then, turning to Chef Perry, she added, "We're going to need more hot chocolate."

The case, of course, was still empty. Well, technically, it held nitrogen, oxygen, and the other gases that make up our air, but the point was, the goggles were gone.

"I'll need to notify the authorities." Birdie *tsk*ed as she glanced about the room, checking to ensure the letter and other artifacts were in place. "And your parents, of course."

"With this weather, it could be tomorrow before they get here," Nathalie pointed out.

"True." Birdie nodded. "But first, does anyone have anything they'd like to say? If this is a prank, it's not a good one. Now is the time to speak up. Before the detectives arrive."

My insides squirmed like a million worms. Surely

Birdie didn't suspect one of *us*. I knew these girls like I knew basket weaving—not at all—but I couldn't imagine one of them as a crook. . . . Then again, Cassie *had* made that comment about sneaking brownies from her mom's office, *and* she'd disappeared during dinner. I glanced at her with her arms crossed, all smug, and caught Edna glaring at me in return.

"Actually, Birdie, I'd like to report something."

My fingers gripped my Rubik's Cube.

Birdie's eyebrows shot up. "Yes, Edna."

Edna stepped around Cassie to the front. "Well, I was upstairs doing a last-minute sweep, making sure pillows were fluffed and the soap was refilled in the bathroom, and I caught this one here"—she paused and pointed right at me—"snooping around the display case."

Robin and Nathalie gasped. Cassie smirked. Wren frowned. And Thea shook her head.

I, on the other hand, could have barfed on Amelia Earhart's carpet.

"It's not like that, I swear!" Panic filled my chest. What was I even thinking by coming here? I didn't belong in this house, with these people. I wanted out.

"Hold on. Millie was with us, in Amy Otis's room, showing us her Rubik's Cube. Right, Robin?" Wren asked. Robin nodded, too scared to speak. "See?" said Wren. "Ashford had no time to swipe a cent."

I could have hugged them both, though Wren would've punched me in the arm.

Birdie gave me an irritated smile. "Explain."

"I was looking for a bedroom, and the door was unlocked, so I opened it. I about peed my pants when I saw plastic people. Then I spied the goggles in the case, along with the letter to Mr. Fernstorm."

"Fern*strom*," Birdie corrected.

"Yes, Fernstrom. So, I crept closer for a better look, and she"—I nodded to Edna—"yelled that this room was off-limits, even though it was unmarked and unlocked. She kicked me out, then locked the door behind me."

Edna's mouth fell open. "I was doing my *job*. You didn't have any business poking your nose in that room until the scavenger hunt began."

"Enough!" Birdie shouted.

Behind me, Nathalie jumped. Thea fiddled with her scarf.

Wren remained unfazed. "So, the door was locked? Did you *see* Edna lock it?"

I thought back to the moment I headed across the hall and met Robin and Wren. "I guess not." I frowned. "I just heard her keys."

"Regardless of who was in here and why, we need to keep the room sealed off, so the detectives can do their job. The goggles must be in the house, somewhere. Meanwhile, we stay out of this room. Is that clear?"

Everyone nodded.

"Collin?" Birdie asked.

"Yes."

"Dispose of that trap and meet us downstairs. We're going to have a chat."

CHAPTER FIFTEEN

Back in the Otis library, the fire in the hearth had dwindled to a faint glow. Shadows cast from the Christmas tree's branches stretched up the wall like ghostly fingers. The air had a chill to it. A sense of foreboding. I shivered and pulled my jacket around me. No one spoke. Instead, we glanced suspiciously at one another. Edna volunteered to stoke the fire. With every mad jab, she created a burst of embers and ash. I didn't breathe until she'd placed the white-hot poker back on its stand. That woman was as tense as a rubber band. Mom said, when it came to crises, trust your gut.

My gut didn't trust Edna.

Dad thought that was a bunch of baloney, by the way. He preferred being prepared so he didn't find himself in sticky situations to begin with. But sometimes, you crash and burn no matter how much you've prepped. Then it's you and your instincts against the world. Maybe I'm being a tad dramatic, but that's exactly how this whole museum experience felt. There was no manual for this. No instruction sheet. No step-by-step guide I could dutifully follow.

This was light-years outside my comfort zone.

Speaking of comfort, Chef Perry had cleared away the cheesecakes and left a steaming pot of hot cocoa and a pile of shortbread cookies. He'd also brewed tea and set out a cheery bowl of fruit. I was somewhat relieved, as I didn't think my nerves could take another chocolate rush. But a cup of sooth-ing tea and a side of buttery cookies? Yes, please.

Nathalie sat beside me on the piano bench. I nibbled on my cookie; she broke a bit of hers off. I sipped my tea and watched as Rosie Stancer stuck her whiskers out of Nathalie's pocket. Rosie's tiny pink nose twitched. She took the cookie crumbs, gnawed on them surprisingly fast, and then disap-peared once again into her temporary home.

On the sofa, Robin was sandwiched between Thea and Wren. Cassie stood a little bit away, inspecting the Christmas tree. She probably knew the exact species and where it had originated.

Birdie didn't even bother to sit down.

"I tried to phone the police, but of course there's no service. Even the gift shop's landline is out. High winds blew down the only phone cable." Birdie clasped her hands together and sighed. "All we can do is stick together, stay alert, and wait."

Wait. *Wait for what?* I wondered. The storm to pass? The thief to confess? The goggles to magically reappear?

Next to me, Nathalie knotted her braid. "Is it just me, or does Grandma Otis's portrait seem angrier at night?"

I wrinkled my nose. "It's not you. She definitely looks creepier. No telling what she's seen and heard."

Nathalie's voice dropped. "Maybe ask if she knows who stole the goggles."

I smiled, then shuddered. We were surrounded by strangers and spooky paintings. In a creaky old house. With a burglar on the loose. I could forget sleeping tonight. I had a tough enough time quieting my brain on normal nights. And this night was so far from normal.

I wished Birdie hadn't taken our devices and, therefore, our flashlights. I thought of Edna, jiggling that basket and demanding my phone. Resentment built up inside me like a shaken can of soda about to explode. I hadn't agreed to come here to be scared, or cut off from contact with the outside world, or literally left in the dark if the power failed. I came here to learn about Amelia. To understand my mother better. To maybe even make new friends. Yes, Collin had brought over extra firewood, but that didn't make me feel any warmer toward him. He'd already spooked me once.

On cue, Collin wandered in and picked the largest orange from the bowl. He pulled a pointy metal tool from his pocket and made an incision into the peel. Then, he expertly slipped the blade underneath the rind to find the fruit's flesh.

Next to me, Nathalie covered Rosie's pocket with her hand. "That's a taxidermist's scalpel," she whispered.

My blood turned cold.

Anyone else would have simply used their fingers. But I was convinced Collin was doing this for show, to creep us out. I cringed as he set the knife down and slurped the fruit straight from its skin.

"Pardon me." He smiled. A dribble of orange juice dripped from his chin.

Birdie passed him a napkin. "You are excused. Please sit down. All of you."

Collin flopped into the chair in the corner, and Cassie perched on the sofa's armrest. Slowly, Birdie sipped her tea and exhaled. She glanced around the room, looking each of us in the face, and asked, "Where do I even start?"

CHAPTER SIXTEEN

Anxiety fluttered in my chest, and I reached for my cube.

"What I'm about to reveal to you is not public information," Birdie began. "The Ninety-Nines, as you know, was founded by Amelia Earhart—"

"She's the one who came up with their name, based on the number of charter members." Nathalie flipped her thick braid over her shoulder and took another bite of shortbread, pocketing the rest.

Wren smirked, and Birdie began again, "Thank you, Nathalie. That is true. Now, back to the story. You see, the organization had long thought that Amelia had hidden something special within this very house."

The hairs on the back of my neck stood up. I stopped

cubing. Something told me I needed to pay close attention.

"How they came to this conclusion, I do not know. Perhaps Amelia hinted at this in one of her many letters, or maybe it was simply hearsay. Gossip. But the item's whereabouts remained a mystery, stumping would-be historians for decades. It was as if the item itself had disappeared into thin air. Then, during a recent renovation, one of the Ninety-Nines discovered . . . a box."

"Oh!" Edna exclaimed as an ornament crashed to the floor. Glass shards glistened in the firelight.

"I'm sorry, Birdie. I was reaching to dust away a cobweb in the corner, and . . ." Edna's cheeks blushed crimson, and she hurried to pick up the pieces.

"No harm done. Girls, be careful of that corner until it's swept."

"I'll grab the broom," Collin said, jumping up.

Birdie nodded to her nephew. "Thank you, Collin. As I was saying, not a single clue had turned up in my many years as caretaker. Until the recent restoration."

"What do you mean by 'restoration'?" I asked.

Birdie sipped her tea and paced the room. "Cosmetic changes. Wallpaper. Floors. Repairing plaster. That sort of thing, in keeping with the original spirit and era of the home. Now, we know Amelia Earhart Putnam moved often, having a residence in Rye, New York, which caught fire, and another in Southern California. At the time of her disappearance, she'd even begun construction on a cabin in Wyoming. But Kansas was Amelia's home, and her grandparents' house represented the happiest years of her childhood. So, when one of our members found a pasteboard art deco box cast aside in storage with boxes of books, magazines, and newspapers from the late 1930s, she didn't think much about it. Any guesses what she found inside?"

"Jewelry?" asked Thea.

"Wads of cash," suggested Wren.

"Secret love letters." Robin sighed and pressed her hands to her heart.

"Her pilot's license!" said Nathalie.

Wren bit off a hangnail. "We're definitely talking dough."

I shook my head and smiled. "Goggles. She found Amelia's goggles."

Birdie's face broke into a grin. "You guessed it, Millie. She found the goggles and the thank-you letter to Mr. Ray Fernstrom, an aerial cinematographer in Hollywood. Apparently, Amelia's goggles had gone missing before."

"As in 'stolen'?" Cassie interrupted.

Birdie shook her head. "Probably misplaced. We have no reason to believe otherwise. Still, Amelia wanted to keep them safe, and she chose here." Birdie's brow furrowed, and her voice turned serious. "Girls, guarding these goggles has been the greatest privilege of my life. If they aren't found before the Smithsonian arrives to collect them, I could lose my job."

Collin returned with the broom, and Wren said, "But, Birdie, if you lose your job, you'd lose your home."

With trembling fingers, Birdie set down her tea. As she did so, the cup rattled in the saucer, and a bit of liquid sloshed onto Electra, curled up on the rug. The cat gave a cranky meow.

"Unfortunately, yes. My home of thirty-five years." Birdie's voice cracked. "I cannot imagine living anywhere else. No one knows this old house like I do. This is the only home Electra's ever known."

Electra's ear twitched at her name, and Birdie gave her furry head a quick scratch. "I'm not getting any younger. This is my home as much as it was Amelia's. No one cares about protecting her legacy more than I do."

My heart ached for Birdie. I knew what it was like to move and feel displaced.

"What can we do?" I asked. "How can we help?"

Edna stopped sweeping long enough to listen. Not that I blamed her. Sweeping was, next to dusting, the absolute worst.

"Find the flight goggles," Birdie answered. "We've already lost Amelia. We can't lose her goggles, too."

"Agreed," said Wren. "But how? The thief has to be one of us."

Unease rippled through the room. Wren said what we had all been thinking. Weren't we all fans of Amelia? I couldn't imagine who here would do such a thing. Then a sick realization hit my gut. Edna had seen *me* admiring the goggles. I was the last person to view them in their display case. That made me, Millie Ashford, the prime suspect.

Quickly, I formulated a plan.

"Birdie, let's conduct our own search. The goggles were here. I saw them myself. We can buddy up, check each other's rooms and luggage. Together, we'll cover every inch of this house."

"Ooh. A systematic search," Nathalie piped up. "I like it. I'm rather good at them, thanks to Rosie."

"You mean Houdini," Wren deadpanned.

Nathalie ignored her. "Working in pairs will keep us honest, too."

"Exactly," I said, sitting up. "The adults can take the common areas—the parlor, the library, the dining room, and the kitchen—while we cover upstairs."

Birdie's face brightened. "I like it. Good thinking, girls. You'll make fine pilots someday."

I gave Birdie a tight-lipped smile. I got dizzy just thinking about maneuvering a hunk of metal thousands of feet above the ground. Though not as dizzy as being suspected of theft . . .

"Ow!" Birdie grimaced and motioned to her side. "Don't mind me. Just an old stomach cramp."

"Are you okay?" I asked.

Birdie waved. "I think so. This happens from time to time."

"Don't worry, Birdie. We can take care of ourselves. You stay by the fire and rest." Wren sounded more confident than I felt.

"Should we keep the same teams as before?" asked Cassie.

"Sounds good to me," I replied, not having the foggiest idea how disastrous this would turn out.

"Well, come on," Wren bossed. "Let's get this search party started."

The wind whipped around the house, and a big gust howled down the chimney, snuffing our fire clean out.

"Um, what was that?" Goose bumps dotted my forearms.

"You guys," said Thea. "Is there a ghost? You know my feelings on ghosts."

A shiver shot up my spine while a snow-filled branch snapped, cracked, and crashed outside.

Cassie backed away from the window. "Yikes! That maple could have killed someone."

Nathalie grabbed my hand. "I don't have a good feeling about this."

I gulped. "I know."

This wasn't a ghost. This was a sign. A sign something bad was about to happen.

"It's all right," Birdie began, holding her forehead. "There shouldn't be any heavy limbs over the roof. Excuse me, I'm feeling a twinge light-headed. Collin, will you please light another fire? I may head upstairs."

Birdie took one step, then sank onto the edge of her armchair.

"Birdie?" Robin asked, leaping up. "Are you okay? Would you like a cookie or more tea?"

Birdie shook her head, and Electra, who had been catnapping at her feet, pounced.

"Rosie!" I pointed just as Rosie Stancer scurried across the floor.

Nathalie screamed.

A door banged open. And the whole house grew dark.

CHAPTER SEVENTEEN

"Everyone stay calm." Chef Perry's voice came from the direction of the door. "I'll reset the circuit breakers."

"Rosie!" Nathalie wailed again.

"If we had our phones, we would have *flashlights*."

Wren. I could have laughed were the circumstances not so tense. Naturally, she was mad that Birdie had locked up our devices. We all were. And now there was a rogue rodent on the loose and a cranky cat.

"I'll get candles," said Edna.

"I'll find a flashlight," said Collin.

The pair fumbled their way out of the room into the dark.

"Well, I'm not moving an inch until it's safe," I said. This night was growing more and more intense.

Thud. Something solid hit the floor next to my foot.

"I'm moving! I'm moving!" I sprang from the bench and practically fell onto Thea's lap.

"Um. What was that noise?" asked Thea.

"Someone probably bumped the end table," Cassie replied, though her usual cool-as-a-cucumber voice was taut.

"Ow. I think someone stepped on my toe." Robin let out a moan.

"Well, none of us can see past our own noses. It's like a black hole in here," Wren griped.

Nathalie groaned. "Who cares about a tiny toe when my rat is running for its life?"

"Did someone say 'rat'?" Collin's voice boomed from the doorway. I shuddered. What a creep. "I found a flashlight," he said, "but the, ah, batteries are dead."

Of course. That's been our luck.

Then a match hissed in the dark. Shadows lurked across Edna's face as she reached for a thick candlestick on the mantel. I wished she didn't look so sinister while holding it. Still, light was light. I snatched the candle off the piano behind me. Edna lit it and another before shaking out the match.

"I'll find more," Collin offered.

"How kind of you." Edna passed him a candle. As it traveled, the flame briefly illuminated a bulky shape on the floor. "Now, about this rodent . . ."

"Wait." I grabbed Collin's arm and lowered my light to the ground. "Robin," I whispered. "Someone didn't step on your toe. They collapsed on it."

For there, at everyone's feet, lay Birdie.

CHAPTER EIGHTEEN

"Birdie! Birdie!" Edna rolled her boss onto her back.

"Wake up, Birdie. Wake up!" Collin shook his aunt's shoulders, gently at first, then with more force. But Birdie would not wake up.

I'd performed this skit with Dad and Danni a hundred times in his first aid class. But this—this was real. I didn't have time to be nervous. I had to act.

I looked at Collin. "Call 911."

"There's no service," said Wren.

"I know that!" I snapped. "But we have to try." I dropped to my knees and put my ear to Birdie's face.

A breath of air tickled my cheek. Then another.

"She's breathing," I said, rocking back on my heels. "She's breathing!"

"Thank God." Robin started to cry.

Collin wiped his forehead on his sleeve. His phone was still in his hand.

Then Birdie let out a snore. A big one.

I laughed in relief. "At least *she's* relaxed. We should move her to her chair."

"If not her bed." Edna lowered a candle, and worry flashed across her face. It was strange Birdie would fall asleep like this, so sudden and fast.

I placed my arms underneath Birdie's and helped Collin hoist her into her chair. "Does Birdie have narcolepsy?" I asked.

Collin shook his head. "Not that I know of."

On cue, Birdie snored again. To put it mildly, she snored like a freight train. It was amazing how much sound could come out of a little body.

"Why I carry earbuds." Collin patted his pocket.

"I hope you have a nose plug, too," I added.

"Millie!" Thea gasped.

"I'm being serious, Thea. Come here."

Up close, Birdie stank. I don't mean she reeked of rosy perfume or too much garlic. I couldn't put my finger on what exactly, but her breath smelled sour. Like sweaty gym socks.

I would have been embarrassed for her had she not already collapsed cold onto the floor.

Thea waved a hand in front of her face. "Phew. I should see if Perry needs help with the power box."

Cassie hugged herself. "Power would be nice."

"Yes, please," Nathalie called from underneath the sofa. She was still searching for her rat. Meanwhile, Electra had disappeared into the dark. Yikes. I hoped for Nathalie's sake that Rosie had hidden somewhere safe.

The lights clicked on before Thea reached the door.

"You should have volunteered sooner," joked Cassie.

Thea wandered over to the gingerbread house and snatched a piece of licorice. "There's always next time," she said with a smirk.

"Next time? Are you trying to jinx us?" asked Robin as Perry appeared, brushing cobwebs from his hair.

"That wasn't too bad. Wait. What's wrong with Birdie? Did she fall?" Perry's face creased with concern.

"Not exactly. Sleeping, is all," answered Edna. She'd covered Birdie's legs with a blanket. "But she'd rest better upstairs."

Collin pulled his arm across his chest, stretching out his shoulder. "I agree one hundred percent. Perry, can you help? I have this old sports injury—a bad rotator cuff—and would hate to hurt myself."

Perry pressed his lips together. Something told me he was annoyed.

"Of course," he said. "The last thing we need is another injury." He smiled, scooped Birdie into his arms, and carried her gently upstairs. Edna followed, jingling the keys to the caretaker's suite.

In turn, Collin fished his phone from his pocket and disappeared into the foyer.

I looked at the girls. "Not to be all dramatic, but—"

Nathalie brushed off her leggings. "Did you see how Collin dodged going upstairs? What was that about?"

"He's probably calling the police!" Robin whispered, her face turning pale.

"I hope so. Birdie couldn't get through to them earlier, and something about this entire evening smells wrong," I said.

"You can say that again," Cassie said, peering into Birdie's teacup. "Look here."

I peeked inside the cup and held my nose. It was pungent, all right, like the locker room after PE. "How could Birdie not smell that?"

"Easy," Cassie said. "Your olfactory sense dulls as you age. That's why old ladies love strong perfume." Cassie picked up the teapot. "Did anyone else have tea?"

"I did," I replied. "But Birdie had her own. See?"

I pointed to an end table nestled next to Birdie's chair. It held a couple of books and a tiny ceramic teapot, the kind used for single servings.

Wren reached out to touch it, and I grabbed her wrist. "Stop. You guys, what if Birdie was—"

"Was what?" Collin asked, slipping back into the room.

An awkward silence engulfed us. I clutched my cube. "I was saying that maybe Birdie was, um, poisoned."

Collin threw his head back and laughed. I shrank three sizes. If I were a turtle, I'd be tucked inside my shell.

"It's not a joke," I mumbled.

"But it's still laughable. Aunt Birdie's as beloved in Atchison as Amelia Earhart herself. She couldn't possibly have an enemy, much less someone who wished her *dead*." Collin mimed, drawing his finger across his throat.

"Sorry. I didn't mean to suggest Birdie had an arch-enemy." My ears burned hot. "I read lots of mysteries, and—"

Nathalie cut me off. "Millie's not jumping to conclusions, Collin. There was a theft first."

"Which has greatly upset my aunt. Stick to reading mysteries, girls, not solving them. If you'll excuse me, I have some studying to do." Collin grabbed his taxidermy book, then pulled his earbuds from his pocket and began unwinding the cord.

Meanwhile, Cassie lifted the lid on Birdie's teapot. Immediately, her nose wrinkled. "Collin, wait. Does Birdie typically make her own tea?"

Collin frowned. "Look, I'm not that great of a nephew. I don't visit often; only when she badgers me for help with her computer. But I know she drinks tea before bed, and has for years. She says it calms her nerves. But if you want to know for sure, ask Edna or Perry."

Wren cleared her throat. "I have a feeling the police will take care of that."

"Oh my goodness," whispered Robin.

"Okay," Wren said. "No one drinks any more tea, not even a sip, until we get to the bottom of this."

"You got that right," said Thea. "And don't touch anything on that table. They'll check for fingerprints."

Cassie dropped the lid with a clang.

CHAPTER NINETEEN

You couldn't have paid me a million dollars to drink any more liquids that didn't come sealed. Not in this house. Nope. Not after this. And even though Collin said Birdie didn't have any enemies, I knew from reading the news that people perform nefarious acts for all sorts of reasons. Whoever swiped Amelia's goggles and drugged Birdie wanted something. But what? And where were they now?

I steadied my breathing and began looking around the room, wondering whom I could trust, when Edna and Perry slipped in.

"She's all tucked in," Edna chirped, moving to collect our dirty cups and saucers. She stopped short of picking any up and, instead, awkwardly turned and twiddled her thumbs. We all understood that everything needed to be left alone for the police. Even so, Perry plucked a pear from the bowl and took a few bites.

"Maybe someone should contact Birdie's doctor," I suggested.

"Good idea." Perry rubbed his forehead and frowned. "Why don't you girls head upstairs to your rooms? Let the adults figure out what's next. I hate to say it, but between the goggles and Birdie's collapse, something sinister may be afoot."

"Hold your horseradish, Chef," blurted Wren. "We are chief witnesses. We are a part of this, like you. You can't send us to our rooms when a suspect is on the loose. We may be minors, but we have seen and heard things too."

Edna sighed. "She's right, Perry. They may be able to help."

Whoa! I couldn't believe my ears. Grumpy Pants was siding with us.

Perry shook his head. "No. I refuse to mix them up in this."

"No disrespect, sir, but we are already mixed in." Thea parked herself on the arm of the couch.

"Like raisins in cookies," said Robin. "It can't be undone."

"Fine." Perry threw up his hands. "Have it your way. But don't come crying to me if you get burned." And he stormed through the doorway and left.

Edna blinked. "He didn't mean that. He's on edge. We all are." She surveyed the mess of saucers and cups. "Don't touch anything." And she followed Perry past the ginger-bread house and on to the kitchen.

"Don't worry. We won't," said Cassie, right before she dipped her finger into Birdie's teacup and placed a drop of liquid on her tongue.

"What are you doing?" asked Nathalie.

"Yeah. I'm not sure that was the best idea," I said, suddenly wishing I was back in the New Horizons Poultry cab with Kate and Dad. This night needed a do-over.

"Stop being such worry warts," said Wren. "It's one drop."

I wanted to ask Wren if it was only one drop then why wasn't *she* trying it too, but I kept my mouth shut.

"Well?" asked Robin.

"Yeah. What's the verdict?" asked Thea.

Cassie licked her lips. "Valerian root. It's an herbal remedy for insomnia and anxiety and has been used for centuries to induce sleep."

"How can you be so sure?" I asked.

Cassie smirked. "Easy. Valerian is instantly recognizable by its sweaty-sock odor."

"Which is why Birdie's breath smelled so bad!" I said.

"Bingo." Cassie nodded. "Valerian root is brewed in tea or sold in capsule form. We've thought of growing it in the NASA greenhouse as an alternative sleeping aid for the astronauts who will travel to Mars. Plant-based pills are better tolerated by the liver and kidneys."

"So, either Birdie drugged herself," Thea mused, "or someone drugged her."

Hearing someone else say those words sent ice coursing through my veins.

Wren bit her lip. "Collin!"

Collin jerked his head up and removed his headphones. "What?"

"Does Birdie have a history of insomnia?"

Collin turned over his taxidermy textbook. The fox in the bow tie glared at me. "Not that I know of. Even if she did, she wouldn't dare take a sleeping pill with you here. She's looked forward to this event for weeks."

Robin shook her head. "Who, then? Who would do this? And who would steal Amelia's goggles?"

"A crazed collector," Collin suggested, picking up his book. "An Amelia fanatic. Maybe someone who knows what those goggles are worth."

The clock on the mantel chimed nine, though it felt more like midnight. A lot had happened in five hours. I stifled a yawn as Nathalie poked around beneath the Christmas tree for Rosie Stancer. "Did anyone see which way Electra went?"

"That reminds me," Cassie said. "Valerian is also a cat-nip! Remember when Electra went bonkers earlier?"

Nathalie grabbed Cassie's arm. "What? She wasn't acting that way because of Rosie Stancer?"

"I don't know for sure, but valerian definitely makes cats

go bananas. Interestingly, it's also used as bait for rodents."

"That's funny, because Collin was setting rattraps upstairs," added Robin.

"That's right!" Nathalie swiveled around, her braid slicing the air. "If you poison my pet rat . . ."

"Hold on!" Collin put his hands up. "Valerian doesn't poison them. It only lures them in. They like the scent. They smell it, enter the box through a one-way door, and can't get back out. I set them free outside. It's as humane a process as there is."

Nathalie took a gulp of air. "If Electra hasn't found her first."

"You really should get a tracker for this rat of yours. I could help with that, you know," Thea said, fiddling with her scarf.

Nathalie glared at her. "Timing, Thea. Have you ever heard of it?"

Thea shrugged. "Only a suggestion, friend. No one's trying to make enemies here."

Collin looked at his book, then back at us. "I'm going to check on my aunt and try to sleep a bit. We'll have a busy morning when the police arrive for questioning."

"Collin, what are the goggles worth, exactly?" asked Wren.

"Beats me." Collin shrugged. "But I'd guess a lot."

I waited for Collin to leave before speaking. "Kate with

New Horizons told me she heard they were worth over one hundred grand."

Cassie whistled. "A collector would know for certain. I've met some crazy collectors at my parents' fund-raisers. But the truth is, we know very little about the museum staff and one another."

"And what we do know could be exaggerated or false," I said, glancing down at my cube. Drat; an edge piece was flipped.

Wren picked up a vase on the mantel, peered inside, and then put it back. "In other words, *everyone* is a suspect."

"Everyone." Robin dramatically flopped back onto the settee. Her messy bun was growing messier by the minute.

Thea scanned the room. "The thief is here, all right. Under this roof. The question isn't *where* but *why* and *who*."

I took a deep breath, forcing down the rising anxiety in my chest. "That's what we have to find out."

CHAPTER TWENTY

Robin pushed her glasses higher on her nose. "And how are we going to find the thief? We can't even find Nathalie's mouse."

"Rosie's a rat." Nathalie peered underneath the piano. "And I'm not leaving without her." She hopped up and dusted off her hands. "Did you know rats possess episodic memories and can recall specific events?"

"Cool. I wish she were here to recall who swiped Amelia's goggles." Cassie crossed her arms.

"Me too." Nathalie picked up a pillow on the sofa, sighed, and set it back down. "They could both be any-where."

Wren popped her knuckles. "Think back to where each of us was earlier in the evening. That could give us a clue as to who took the goggles and when. For starters, we know Millie saw them before dinner."

"True. Until Edna yelled that I wasn't supposed to be there and kicked me out."

Robin cocked her head to the side. "Do you think she took the goggles, then?"

I shrugged. "She could have, but she was so nice to us just now."

Thea narrowed her eyes. "She could be acting."

"It all could be acting!" Robin blurted.

"Well, no one's pretending Rosie's missing," Nathalie snapped. "She could be in real danger, you know."

"Same," said Wren.

Cassie brushed her bangs out of her eyes. "Focus, people. We *all* could be in danger."

Robin wrung her hands. "Maybe we should run next door. You know, ask for help."

I swallowed. "I thought of that, but Birdie told me earlier that her neighbors were either away for the holidays or had left town to beat the storm."

Wren looked at the ceiling. "So, we're on our own."

"Yeah." I bit my lip.

Thea nodded. "Okay. If Edna didn't take the goggles, someone else could have when we were busy unpacking. Or when we were all together in the dining room downstairs."

"Thea's right," Robin said. "But we should think beyond the house staff."

"Wait a minute," Cassie said. "Is this about my getting Robin's meds at dinner? Because I'm not a crook!"

"No one is saying you are," I said. "We just need to be open to the possibility that the thief could be anyone."

Cassie pursed her lips. "Well, *you* were the last one to see the goggles."

My heart beat fast. "Wow. That's not what I meant."

"Edna saw you by the case, Millie." Robin sat up on the sofa. "You can't blame us for having suspicions."

I shut my eyes. They had every right to wonder about me.

"Your room is directly across from the goggles. Who's to say you or Wren didn't sneak over after I moved down the hall?" I asked.

Robin looked hurt. "First of all, that's ridiculous. Second, you said yourself that Edna locked the room."

"I think she did." I rubbed my forehead. "It's all a blur."

"And honestly, what would Wren and I do with Amelia's goggles?" asked Robin.

"Easy. An exclusive video," said Wren. "Just think of all our new subscribers."

We stared at her.

"I'm kidding! *Kidding*." Wren put up her hands. "It was a joke."

"A bad one," said Nathalie.

"Yeah, okay," said Wren, "but tell me where you were when we first went upstairs."

"Nathalie was looking for Rosie Stancer in the common area. I saw her," I said.

"She's still looking," said Wren. "Unless she's using her missing rat as an excuse to case the place."

"I'm doing no such thing, Wren Winters. Rosie is family." Wounded, Nathalie stuck out her chin.

"You were awfully quick to ask Birdie about the goggles," added Cassie.

"Because they're what everyone wants to see!" Nathalie threw her hands up in disgust. "I can't believe this. And Cassie! You stole brownies from NASA's test kitchen. Why should I believe you'd stop there?"

Cassie fussed with the flower in her hair. "A raging sweet tooth has a mind of its own."

"Guys, I see a couple of motion sensors." Thea pointed to the walls. "Did anyone notice security cameras upstairs?"

"No," I said, thankful for the change of topic. "But I wasn't looking for any."

"I didn't," said Wren.

"No." Cassie pouted and crossed her arms in a huff. An awkward silence followed.

Wren sighed. "I know things are tense, but we need to work together. We need to find the goggles. Before one of us is next."

"Is what? Drugged?" asked Robin.

"Well, that's morbid," said Cassie.

"No, it's probable." I shoved my cube back into my pocket. "Statistically speaking, burglars return to the scene of the crime. If the same holds true for all criminals, each of us has an eleven percent chance of becoming the next victim."

Silence.

"I don't know about you, but that's eleven points too high for me." Cassie pulled the flower from her hair and rolled its base between her fingers. "If a zinnia can beat all odds to bloom in microgravity, we can beat this. I'm not going to become some statistic." She put the flower back above her ear.

"Neither are we," said Wren, heading for the stairs. "*We* have an advantage."

"We do?" asked Robin.

Thea crossed her arms and smirked. "We're younger, smarter, and at least one of us has practiced martial arts."

"Okay, that was me, in kindergarten," said Robin.

Wren reached the first step, turned around, and smiled. "All correct, Thea. But you missed an important part. There's one of them, and six of us."

"The *Amelia* Six," I said, standing up.

Thea grinned. "Yeah, yeah. Let's find some goggles."

Once we'd reached the landing, I found myself giving orders. This surprised me, as I'm not the bossy type—that's my mother—but strategy? Strategy was my specialty. We needed a plan of attack. With only one night to search this house crammed with artifacts, we had to make the most of our time.

"Wren and I will take the spare bedroom," I began. "Thea and Nathalie, you take Amelia's room. Robin and Cassie, you've got Amy Otis's room. Check bags, dressers, closets, desks, underneath the beds. Don't leave any picture frame unturned. If nothing shows up upstairs, we'll move down." I paused and looked each girl in the face. It was hard to believe any of them could be a thief. "Let's get detecting."

Wren flipped on the light switch to the guest bedroom. "I'll check your bag while you search Thea's."

"Okay. I don't have much," I said, studying Thea's stuffed backpack. I was my father's daughter: too practical for my own good.

I unbuckled the flap on Thea's bag and found a rolled-up hoodie, sweatpants, chargers, a battery pack, toiletry bag, one of those multi-tools, duct tape, and a clean black shirt. No goggles, other than the motorbike ones she wore in. I frowned and shoved everything back inside. Her headphones still rested on the nightstand, with the cord carefully wound. Funny; she didn't strike me as a neat freak.

"This feels icky, invading someone's privacy." I made my way to Cassie's overnight bag, the one with the huge mono-grammed *C*.

"We reached an agreement and shook on it. Do you want to find the goggles or not?" Wren slid out a dresser drawer. "Empty." She looked disappointed.

"Don't be silly. Of course I want to find them. I guess I don't like snooping." I sank onto the bed and unzipped Cassie's bag, revealing her belongings: polka-dotted pajamas, a sleep mask, jeans, cozy socks, a gray sweatshirt, and another tin box.

"Hold up," Wren said. "What's that?"

"What's what?" I asked, lifting the lid to the box. Colorful candy in shiny wrappers filled the inside like confetti. I thought back to Cassie's comment about my Twizzlers and laughed. "So much for artificial colors and preservatives."

"Uh-huh," Wren said. She picked up Cassie's sweatshirt and stared at the gold letter P on the front.

"What?" I asked.

"That's Purdue's logo."

"Oh. Right." The letter looked familiar, like I'd seen it recently, but I couldn't place where. "Maybe she knows someone there."

"Maybe." Wren paced back and forth. She poked her head under both beds and peered around the bedside table. "Still, we should show the others."

"Okay. But why?"

"Why?" Wren repeated. "Because Cassie's now the number-one suspect."

CHAPTER TWENTY-ONE

Moments later, we'd all piled onto the twin beds.

"What's this about?" Robin asked, pulling her knees up to her chest. "Cassie and I only checked the trunks." Thea and Nathalie plopped down next to her, looking equally confused.

"We found something in Cassie's luggage," I replied.

"They found a shirt." Cassie rolled her eyes.

Wren waved the Purdue shirt in front of her face. "Cassie. This is serious."

Cassie laughed. "Birdie collapsing is serious. A smelly college sweatshirt is not."

Then it hit me, what Kate had said in the New Horizons Poultry truck. That some big university had made a move to house the goggles for their collection. *Whoa.* And now I remembered that Amelia had been on the faculty at Purdue

University in Indiana. *Wait a second.* Cassie was from Indiana. Or was it Houston? My brain whirred to connect the dots. Could Cassie be linked to Purdue and the goggles' disappearance?

"Go ahead. Search the whole room if you want." Cassie crossed her arms in annoyance. "But you won't find a thing. I didn't do it. I don't know who stole Amelia's goggles. A true fan wouldn't steal. Only a deranged one."

It was Wren's turn to scowl.

"We searched. And you're right. We didn't find the goggles. Still, you need to tell us your connection with the university," Wren said. "Anyone with any access to the Internet or TV knows that Purdue and the Smithsonian have been fighting over those goggles. And Purdue lost."

Nathalie sucked in a breath.

Cassie sighed. "I know. I know it looks bad, but I'm on your team, all right? The shirt belonged to my dad."

Wren handed the shirt back. "What do you mean, 'belonged'?"

Cassie sniffed the fabric, and her face softened. "Dad had leukemia. He died when I was three."

"I'm so sorry." I placed my hand on her arm.

She gave me a sad smile. "Thanks. The man you saw earlier is my stepfather. Anyway, my parents met at Purdue when they were nineteen. Mom asked me to take a picture of the goggles. That's all, I swear."

Wren's lip twitched. She believed Cassie—right?

Cassie kept on. "Purdue paid for Amelia's around-the-world airplane, the Electra."

"Including all modifications. Amelia replaced the ten passenger seats with extra fuel tanks and a navigation station," said Robin.

"Exactly. The Electra 10-E was Amelia's 'flying laboratory.' Unfortunately, they both disappeared."

"Wow." Thea whistled.

"Speaking of disappearing," Wren began, "were you able to get a picture of the goggles?"

Cassie's smile slipped. "Ugh. No. That's why I offered to get Robin's medicine at dinner. But I didn't know which part of the house they were in, and I chickened out. Then Birdie took away our devices."

"Don't remind me," said Thea.

Cassie smirked. "Well, I could have hugged her. My parents can be so suffocating. They tell me what to wear. What to eat. What classes to take at school. Maybe I don't want to become a big-shot architect or engineer like them. What if I want to be an artist? Or a musician? Or live on a flower farm?"

I thought of Kate, and a warm feeling blossomed in my chest.

"I mean, if I can intern at NASA, great. But I want to do it on my terms. Not theirs. I'm not the rocket scientist they think I am. I like gardening and"—she touched the zinnia in her hair and grinned—"watching things grow."

The longer I listened to Cassie, the more I believed her. She hadn't swiped the goggles. But someone had. Still, these dresser drawers sat empty. There was nothing but dust bunnies underneath the beds. And all I'd found in the nightstand was a stubby pencil.

"Sorry we suspected you, Cassie," I said.

She cocked her head. "It's okay. We should keep searching, though. We're running out of time."

Robin checked her watch. "If we're finished here, we could use help across the hall in Amy Otis's room."

Wren looked at me and shrugged. "Sure."

"We'll be there as soon as Thea clears Amelia's room of ghosts." Nathalie winked. Thea shook her head, and in spite of all the no-good, horrible events of this evening, I smiled. A few quick turns on my cube—right, left, right—and I'd made a wish. Two wishes, in fact. One, that we'd find the goggles, and two, that Rosie Stancer would reappear.

I still didn't care for rodents. But I liked Nathalie. And, like her and Cassie, I knew how it felt to miss someone special. It felt like a hole smack dab in the center of your heart.

Across the hall, Cassie rummaged through Wren's bag. I knew it belonged to Wren, as Wren's arms were crossed, and she was rolling her eyes more than usual.

"I told you. You aren't going to find anything. We're wasting our time searching one another's bags."

This was starting to sound all too familiar.

"You don't know that for sure," Robin replied as I turned her satchel upside down, spilling its contents on Amy Otis Earhart's bed. Robin watched as I sorted through her pajamas, lip gloss, half a dozen gel pens, Mars Millennium merch, and two tattered journals.

"All clear," I announced.

Robin picked up a Mars Millennium button and tossed it to me.

"Thanks!" I said, catching the shiny metal disc.

"Clear here, too." Cassie sighed and backed away from Wren's bag.

"Told you," Wren said. "A waste of time."

Not wanting to get in the middle of a sibling dispute, I studied the holographic image of the Red Planet with its superimposed *M*. Was the *M* for "Mars"? "Millennium"? Or both? I shrugged and tacked the planet to my shirt, next to Mom's pin and my new Amelia Six one.

Robin admired my collection. "The *M* could be larger, don't you think?"

"I like it," I said.

Robin smiled. "Thanks. We should interview you on our site. Right, Wren? Millie could talk about speedcubing."

"Totally. But let's find these goggles first." Wren slammed

her suitcase shut then stood on top of it to reach a high shelf.

Across the room, Cassie searched a cupboard. "Don't forget the closets."

"An original Rubik's Cube did go to space," I said.

Robin put her belongings away. "Really?"

"Yeah. Canadian astronaut David Saint-Jacques supposedly took his childhood puzzle to the International Space Station." I peered inside Amelia's desk as goose bumps tickled my arms. "Imagine the letters written here."

Robin hugged her journal. "Everyone, I feel a new haiku: Secret wishes breathed/to life on scraps of paper/airplanes in the wind."

"Knock, knock." Thea appeared in the doorway. "Nothing in Amelia's room."

"Nada." Nathalie shuffled in, her shoulders drooped in defeat. She looked like her best friend had gone missing. Which maybe she had.

Sensing her sadness, Robin asked, "Nathalie, do you mind if I look through your bag? Yours is the last one."

Nathalie motioned for her to go ahead. "Sure." Robin nosed through Nathalie's things and held up a pack of cards. Nathalie shook them out onto the floor. Each one had a photograph of an endangered animal stamped on the back. There were rhinos, frogs, seals, monkeys, and more. It was depressing to think of these beautiful animals at risk.

"Every one of them has a story," said Nathalie. "Just like us."

A thought came to me as I opened my dozenth dresser drawer. *The thief has a story too.* It was my job to listen for it.

"Guys, we're thinking about this all wrong. We need to think like a thief. If we were criminals, what would we do with a pair of goggles?" I asked.

Robin sat on the edge of the bed. "Hmm. The goggles are too bulky to hide in a pocket and too unique to wear. We'd stash them somewhere. Maybe inside a mattress."

Nathalie's head snapped up. Her eyes shined bright. "Exactly. I once found Rosie sleeping inside my shoe. We need to think outside the box. Somewhere no one would ever guess."

Wren sighed. "If only we knew where that was." Then she threw open the wardrobe and screamed.

CHAPTER TWENTY-TWO

Wren screamed. I screamed. We all screamed as a body fell out of the wardrobe and hit the floor. It made a horrible, lifeless thud.

Thea and I held on to each other like the floor was hot lava. We were, as my dad would say, being ridiculous. But I'd never seen a dead body before.

Neither had the others, apparently.

"Ashford! Pull yourself together. It's a mannequin, not a murder victim," said Wren.

I stopped flailing and stared. Thea caught her breath too, as did everyone else who wasn't made of plastic. As sure as the sun is hot, Wren was right. Someone had moved one of the mannequins from the artifacts room into this old armoire.

I turned the figure over and gasped. It wore a flight cap

and goggles identical to the ones Birdie gave us. But the most chilling detail was the museum postcard pinned to its chest using Collin's scalpel.

With trembling fingers, I pulled the blade out and flipped the card over. On the reverse side, someone had scrawled in ink:

Dear Mr. Fernstrom:
Tell those kids to stop snooping. Or else.

"Or else?" I gulped.

"I smell a rat," Thea said.

"Really? Did you have to say 'rat'?" wailed Nathalie.

"Guys, this scavenger hunt is nothing like what they promised in the invitation. I want to go home." Robin's voice broke right as Collin rushed into the room. His face was flushed, and he was short of breath.

"We heard screams. Is everyone all right?"

"This mannequin dove out of the armoire and scared the pants off us. But otherwise we're fine," I said.

Collin rubbed his chin. "Just jumped out, huh?"

"With this." I held out the scalpel.

All color left Collin's face. He grabbed his instrument and inspected it. "Where'd you find this?"

Wren pointed back to the mannequin while Collin checked each of his pockets.

"Is this someone's idea of a joke?" His voice grew tense.

His eyes scanned the room from one corner to the next. He poked around under the bed and checked inside the wardrobe.

"If so, it's a sick one," Cassie said.

Collin put his hands on his hips and took two calming breaths. "Listen. I understand you girls are away from your parents and having fun, but this nonsense needs to stop. Now." A vein popped out on his forehead.

I shook my head, trying to understand what he was implying. "Collin, we aren't the ones who did this."

"Someone is trying to scare *us*," Wren said. "Don't you see? This note is worded like the Fernstrom letter from the display case. . . . Plus, we're the kids here."

"Smart ones, too," he added, moving the mannequin to the corner. "Everyone in this house is officially a suspect until those goggles turn back up." He wiped his face, and I noticed his hands shook. He had to feel somewhat responsible for us, with Birdie out of commission for the night. "It's probably best if you girls get ready for bed. If you need anything, I'll be in the library. I need time to think. Edna will bring up a tray of snacks."

No one said a word as he left.

"I don't know about you, but there's no way I can go to sleep right now. I want to get to the bottom of this," I said.

"Same. And look here." Nathalie pointed inside the wardrobe. "A crushed peppermint. Someone's been in our room. This could be a clue."

"Leading to some hungry ghost!" Poor Thea. She was obsessed.

"Oh," said Robin. "This is not good. Not good at all."

"Look. This isn't summer camp or time for practical jokes. We could be in real danger," I said, my voice shaking.

"Millie's right," Wren began. "We can't keep secrets. If you know something, you need to speak up. No judgment. We're in this together, for better or"—she looked at the mannequin and gulped—"worse."

I flipped the card over and read the words again. *Or else.* Someone was trying to keep us from snooping. But who?

CHAPTER TWENTY-THREE

Wren walked to the window and stared into the Otises' backyard.

"I know Collin said to go to bed, but we can't sit in this room all night," she said.

"Especially with that mannequin in the corner," Robin said with a shudder.

"Agreed," Nathalie said. "Not with Rosie loose. She must be so scared, being lost in this creaky old house."

Time ticked by. Robin browsed every book on the shelf. Thea hummed every song. I solved my cube. Solved it again. Anything to quiet the anxious thoughts looping in my head. *We'll never get out of here. We'll never find the goggles. What would Mom think? I miss Dad. Stop snooping. Or else.*

"We never finished the scavenger hunt. I so would have won," Cassie said with a sigh.

Wren snorted. "Please. Millie and I were way ahead."

"No way," said Thea. "Cassie and I had so many items checked off."

"Not as many as we did. Remember when we saw Perry in the butler's pantry? *We* were practically done," I said, picking up a framed photograph.

"Hmpf." Thea took Nathalie's playing cards and started shuffling. I studied the black-and-white candid of Amelia, dressed in a bell hat and pleated skirt. She leaned on an open-cockpit biplane. Her left hand was hooked onto the propeller, and her right hand, planted on her hip, gripped a pair of goggles. Not *the* goggles, but still cool.

Thea fanned the cards on the floor. "Hey, Millie, pick one."

"Okay," I said, hardly glancing at the two of hearts I'd chosen. I was too busy squinting at this picture and its caption. *Famed Flyer Amelia Earhart makes an emergency landing in her Avro Avian and uses silk stocking to filter fuel. McNeal, AZ, 1928.* I barely made out the markings painted in bold type on the airplane's tail: *G-EBUG.* Wait a minute. I was almost certain I'd seen those letters before.

On Chef Perry's arm.

"You guys." I rushed to fill them in on my discovery.

Thea scooped up her cards. "What do you mean 'Perry's tattoo'?"

I explained again and showed her the picture.

"Big deal. He has Amelia's plane tattooed on his forearm," Cassie said.

"Well, if I was going to get a tattoo honoring Amelia Earhart, I would choose either the red Vega or the Electra," I said.

"Ditto," said Nathalie.

"Well, I'd pick the *Friendship*," said Robin. Yeah, Robin was a total Hufflepuff.

Wren frowned. "Why would he choose one of her lesser-known planes?"

"Beats me," I said. "I almost asked him about it, but I wanted to win the scavenger hunt, and then we found that secret passageway."

Thea arched an eyebrow. "Excuse me?"

"Secret passageway? What secret passageway?" Robin's mouth dropped open.

Wren grinned. "There's a hidden passageway that connects the gift shop to the hallway upstairs. Millie and I stumbled onto it looking for scavenger hunt answers."

Thea waved her hands in the air. "Stop right there. First of all, you didn't think to tell us? Hello? And second, ghosts love secret passageways. The narrower and twistier the better. It's like their own amusement park. Find a house with a secret passage, get free scares all day long."

"No ghosts, Thea," I said. "Cross my heart."

"Well, I want to see this passageway for myself," said Robin. "In the daytime."

Nathalie raised her hand. "Me too. Rosie could be hiding there. If not in the kitchen, near the food."

I smiled. "Funny, because that is exactly where I think we should go next."

"The kitchen?" asked Cassie.

I scrambled my cube. "Yeah. To talk to Chef Perry."

"Oh, I don't have a good feeling about this." Robin paced back and forth. "Collin said we're not supposed to leave our rooms."

I smirked. "He won't find out. That's what makes the passageway secret."

"What if we split up?" Cassie stood up. "Three of us can stay here in case Edna checks on us. Three can explore."

Robin looked at us like we'd lost our minds. Maybe we had. But doing nothing would only make my anxiety worse. I looked around the bedroom at Amelia's writing desk, her hope chest, her framed headlines and photographs. Amelia Earhart didn't sit around waiting; she made things happen.

And I would too. "I'm in."

"All right, all right," Wren said. "I can't stand anyone having fun without me. I'll go."

"Me too." Nathalie smiled. It was the first real smile I'd seen on her since Rosie disappeared.

I grinned at them both. "Thanks."

After it was decided who was going (me, Nathalie, Wren) and who was guarding our space (Thea, armed with a broomstick; Cassie; and Robin), I nervously stuffed a Twizzler into my mouth and rubbed my mom's pin for good luck.

"Follow me and stay close," Wren whispered. My insides felt like goo, but I gave her a thumbs-up.

We inched down the hall single file. Wren, then Nathalie, then me, the caboose. Behind me, a radiator hissed to life, and my heart leapt into my throat.

Relax, Millie. It's only the heater.

Seconds later we reached the potted plant. So far, so good. I ran my hand along the wallpaper, looking for the latch.

"There!" Wren pointed.

I lifted the clasp, and the door swung inward.

Nathalie gasped. "Incredible! I bet we'll see some spiders," she murmured. "Arachnids get such a bad rap. They're crucial to our ecosys—"

"Shh, not now." I motioned her inside. The door clicked back into place, and darkness engulfed us. "Don't move until we find the light," I whispered. "You could fall down the stairs."

"Found it," said Wren, and a faint glow, like moonbeams, illuminated the dark. Dim light was better than none. We let our eyes adjust, then Wren led the way.

Fourteen steps in all and eight paces across the pantry-like space at the bottom. But there was something I hadn't noticed the first time I stepped through the door, and that was the little rays of light peeking through. I stood on my tiptoes and peered through the knotholes in the wood, straight into the cozy gift shop. I saw the vibrant shelf of neatly stacked souvenir mugs, the postcard rack, glossy Amelia posters and books, cheap museum magnets, touristy tees, keychains, and, in the far corner, blocking the old kitchen service window, an outdated computer.

The door leading into the kitchen was ajar. Chef Perry stood at the sink, shaking ice cubes into a plastic bag. He reached up to grab a towel off his shoulder, and I saw it. The tattoo.

"Should we go talk to him?" I asked, realizing we didn't even have a plan. "I'll say I'm dying of thirst."

"Good thinking." Wren put her palms on the door to push it open, and I grabbed her shoulder.

"Wait!" I whispered.

Footsteps fell on the floorboards as Collin cut through the gift shop and into the kitchen. *Whew.* That was close.

Collin said hi to Perry, popped open a can of soda, and took a big swig. My right leg started to tingle, so I shifted my weight to the other foot. How real detectives survived hours-long surveillance was beyond me. Snacks would definitely help.

Perry scoured the spice cabinet for an ingredient while Collin opened the freezer door. He must have said something funny, because Perry laughed. Then Collin closed the door and left. I couldn't tell if he was searching for something, hiding something, or had simply wanted a midnight snack. That's when it hit me. These weren't knotholes in the door.

They were peepholes. Holes someone drilled. We hadn't seen them for all the artifacts displayed on the other side. Maybe they'd been here since the slave trade. When the gift shop had been a kitchen, the heart of the home, and the home had served as a sanctuary for enslaved people heading north.

"Wren." I scooted over.

"What is it?" she asked.

"Look," I whispered, and motioned to the hole. As I did, Edna carried her cleaning caddy into the shop. She straightened a wayward souvenir mug on the shelf, waved to Perry in the kitchen, and then crossed the room, plopping her supplies down right in front of us.

She popped something into her mouth and pulled on a pair of rubber gloves. *Drat.* We couldn't sneak into the kitchen if Edna was working in the gift shop. She'd spot us immediately.

"What now?" Nathalie whispered.

Wren, still spying, waved her hand for silence. I peeked through the hole in time to see Edna look up, check the hallway entrance, then look back over her shoulder into the kitchen.

That's strange.

Wren must have thought so too, because she put a death

grip on my arm. I stifled a yelp while Edna pulled three large sheets of newsprint from the bottom of the caddy, along with another object. Something solid. That's when my breath caught.

Edna had Birdie's teacup.

She paused and brought her watch up to her mouth.

"What's she doing?" I asked. "This is tampering!"

"Shh," Wren whispered.

Edna began talking into her watch.

At first, her words were muffled; then she grew agitated.

"What about the girls?" she hissed. "I'm calling . . . Stuart. I'm not playing."

Stuart? Who was Stuart? And why did she need to call him? And what did this have to do with us?

The three of us stood transfixed on the other side of the wall as Edna wrapped Birdie's cup in layers of paper. She quickly boxed the bundle up and buried it in the bottom of her caddy, beneath a pile of rags.

"Oh my gosh. She's hiding the evidence!" I looked to Nathalie and Wren.

Edna picked up her feather duster like nothing had happened. Nothing at all.

My head spun and my heart beat fast. I'd prepared my whole life for this moment, solving a real-life mystery. So why did I feel like throwing up? I rolled my Rubik's Cube in my hand. "We need to tell the others."

✳ ✳ ✳

Back in Amy Otis's bedroom, Wren, Nathalie, and I described what we'd seen.

"I never liked Edna," Robin said, slamming her journal shut. "You can't trust a housekeeper who doesn't dust."

"She still hasn't brought up those snacks. And did you see how she dropped that Christmas ornament when Birdie first mentioned the goggles?" Thea asked.

Cassie rubbed her forehead. "We have to tell Birdie. Edna could have the goggles hidden in her caddy, too."

"Or Collin. He was digging around in the freezer," Wren added.

"Are you sure he wasn't searching for ice cream?" Robin shrugged. "Or one of his taxidermy projects?"

"Ha," Wren said. "And no. I didn't get a good look."

"Please, no taxidermy jokes." Nathalie's face fell.

"Sorry. Did you see anything else?" Robin asked.

I shook my head. "No, but now that I think on it, Perry was making an ice pack."

Thea looked alarmed. "An ice pack for an injury?"

"Do you think it could be for Birdie?" I asked.

"Maybe," Nathalie said. "Remember, earlier Collin complained about carrying Birdie because of his bad shoulder?"

"Interesting," Cassie said. "A torn rotator cuff is a common baseball injury."

"Huh. He *is* wearing baseball socks," added Wren.

"What?" I asked.

"Yeah. You didn't notice when we looked at his boot print in Amelia's room? He's wearing black-and-gold Purdue baseball socks."

I sank down onto the bed. "I knew I'd seen their logo somewhere else tonight! Maybe he went to school there."

"Or he's a huge fan. He told Birdie she should have donated the goggles to some school, remember? I wish we had a way to look him up. Especially after finding his scalpel like that." Robin shuddered.

"Seriously. We need the Internet," Nathalie said.

"Exactly. Maybe we can try the computer in the gift shop."

"Not with the adults around," said Thea. "We'll have to use Birdie's."

"Birdie has her own computer?" Nathalie asked.

"Yeah, in her apartment. I overheard her tell Collin she needed a new keyboard for her personal computer upstairs." Thea straightened her scarf. "I could probably hack it."

Worry whispered in my ear. "But what if Edna comes to check on us? I don't think we can all leave."

Wren looked at the mannequin still propped in the corner. "Sure we can."

CHAPTER TWENTY-FOUR

I never thought I'd pick my own body double, but here I was, standing in the museum's mannequin room, doing exactly that. Whoever said Atchison, Kansas, was boring was straight-up lying.

"We've got to work quiet and fast," said Wren. "We'll be skunked if Edna catches us carrying these forms. You have two minutes. Find your decoy and get out."

Nathalie chewed on the end of her braid. "It's too much pressure! Do I pick the pilot jacket or the fancy evening gown?"

"It's Amelia Earhart. You can't go wrong," I said, and grabbed the one with the sailor collar. I tried my best not to whack her head on the door frame as I left. *Success!* I unrolled my sleeping bag and zipped Frida in snug as a bug in a rug.

Yeah, I named her. Dad and I always named his work manikins. Plus, it's not every day you can name your replacement.
I turned Frida's head so she was looking away from the door.
Rummaging through my bag, I found my headphones and
slipped them on her for good measure. "Keep the volume
down, or you'll ruin your ears."

On the bed next to me, Cassie was busy tucking in Ms.
Blue Evening Gown. She pulled the covers up to the mannequin's chin and, oh my word, gave her a monogrammed
sleeping mask. Of course she did. Her mannequin, which
remained unnamed, was a big reader. She had no less than
three botany magazines scattered across her bed and one
bottle of nail polish—a shimmery white called On Cloud 9.

Thea, on the other hand, faced her mannequin toward
the wall. She had one pillow under her head and another
covering it.

"She's a light sleeper."

I smiled at her joke. "It's okay. Frida has headphones."

In the other room, Wren and Robin had tucked their
pair into the queen bed. Wren's slept in a beanie, and Robin's
had a box of tissues and a poetry journal open on her chest.
Nathalie's mannequin was settled into her sleeping bag with
a giant plush penguin under her arm. They looked good.
Convincing. Sort of like us.

Something welled up inside me as I looked around at us,
with our Amelia Six pins glinting in the light. Dad would say

it was pride in my preparation. Mom would call it courage, though I didn't feel brave. I felt as fragile as an icicle. But maybe I could be piercing like one too.

"Sleep tight, girls," I said. Then I turned out the lights and left.

A few moments later Robin stood behind me, gripping the back of my shirt. Wren pushed the door open.

"Oh, crumb." The hairs on the back of my neck stood up, and I tiptoed into Birdie's apartment.

My eyes needed a few seconds to adjust to the dark, but my nose worked straightaway. The smell of sweaty socks hit my nostrils. That must have been the valerian.

Luckily, Birdie slept like a baby, tucked snug in her big double bed. On one side of her was a night table with an alarm clock, a glass of water, and a model airplane. And on the other side was a gigantic bookcase that made a cozy office nook, complete with an old desk, the kind where you can lock up the top. Fortunately for us, Birdie had left it open. It held an older computer and a stack of papers. A plump easy chair was positioned in the opposite corner next to a gooseneck floor lamp. A perfect spot for reading. There was also a small kitchenette with a mini fridge, stove, and sink. Then, through a doorway, was a small bathroom done in classic black-and-white tile.

Worry wormed its way through my insides. "I'm not sure we should be here. We could get caught."

Thea sighed. "Or we could find something valuable."

Point taken.

"Look at this!" Robin said softly, pointing to a wall of framed posters.

"Oh wow," I mumbled. "Vintage air show ads."

BE DAZZLED! DELIGHTED! AMAZED!
STELLA "BIRDIE" ANDERSON PERFORMS DAR-ING, DEATH-DEFYING STUNTS.
SCOTT AIR FORCE BASE. JUNE 10–11.

Whoa. Birdie was a stunt pilot? Now that I saw the posters, though, that made sense. Of course Birdie was a pilot and a Ninety-Nine. Why else would she have such a fierce loyalty to the organization and to Amelia's house? Plus, her spunky personality, flashy earrings, and bold lipstick screamed "lime-light."

Robin picked up the model plane on the nightstand. "Do you think this is her plane?" she whispered.

"Guys, focus." Wren waved us over to the desk in the corner. Thankfully, Birdie's computer was powered on, so all Thea had to do was guess the password.

Birdie.

Ninety-Nines.

Amelia Earhart.

Electra.

None worked, but, like an engine, we were just warming up.

"Try Amelia's full name," Nathalie suggested. "Amelia Mary Earhart."

"Or her birthday—July twenty-fourth, 1897," Cassie said.

Thea's fingers clacked across the keyboard. "No luck."

Robin was still across the room studying Birdie's memorabilia. "Try Atchison," she said, walking over to the computer. "Or the address here: 223 North Terrace Street."

"Good ideas," said Thea. "But nope."

I glanced at Birdie, sleeping peacefully, then at the air show posters near her bed. *Be Dazzled! Delighted! Amazed! Stella "Birdie" Anderson* . . .

"Stella. Try 'Stella,'" I said.

Thea's fingers flew.

"Bingo, Millie! We're in." Thea gave me a high five, and I grinned. This wasn't so bad. Then a high-pitched whine turned our bodies to stone.

Nathalie squeezed my arm. "Wh-what was that?"

Thea's hands hovered above the keyboard, and her eyes grew huge. "I don't know, but it's not coming from the computer, and it sounds an awful lot like *ghosts*."

I gulped.

Wren placed a finger to her lips.

Wh-wheee! Wh-wheee! There it was again! My pulse quickened. No one else was in the room with us besides Birdie.

Birdie! I turned around right as Wren let out a laugh.

Birdie had rolled onto her back and begun snoring again! My shoulders sagged with relief.

Thea wiped her forehead. "Thank heavens. Now, let's get cracking." Opening a search engine, she asked, "Where should I start?"

"How about Collin and Purdue?" said Cassie.

Not much turned up, other than a language professor by the same name. Thea added "student" and got a few more hits. But nothing helpful.

"Try adding 'baseball,'" Robin suggested.

"Got it." Thea said, typing "Collin + Purdue + baseball" into the search box. A few seconds later, a dozen-plus hits came back. She clicked on the first one, and I couldn't believe my eyes.

"Are you guys seeing this?" I asked.

"Yeah, but I can't believe it," said Wren.

"Me neither," said Cassie.

"Nor me," said Robin.

"Same," said Nathalie.

Staring at us from the monitor, in a gold baseball uniform, was player #13, Purdue's star pitcher: Collin Ray Stewart. But we knew him only as Collin, Birdie's nephew. He was younger then and wore a full beard.

"Thea, click on another link," said Wren.

"Okay. Here's an alumni article called 'Where Are They Now?'"

We crowded around the monitor to read the text. It was short. And sad. Apparently, Collin had injured his shoulder his senior year, which killed any chance of his turning pro. He then dropped out of school and turned to drinking, followed by a stint in rehab, and now that treatment was behind him, he hoped to become a cop. I looked at the date of the post. Seven years ago.

"Wow." Nathalie whistled. "I guess the whole cop thing didn't work out either."

"Maybe he wants the goggles for cash," I said.

"Maybe. But if he's living in his parents' basement, he shouldn't have many expenses. Unless"—Robin pushed her glasses back onto her nose—"he has a secret baseball card addiction, or his business has gone bankrupt, or he has a mountain of medical bills. Even then, it's still stealing, and a crummy way to treat one's aunt."

On cue, Birdie let out another big snore. Under any other circumstance, I'd have been doubled over, laughing.

"What about Edna?" I asked. "Did you find anything on her?"

Thea shook her head. "No, we don't have a last name, and searching 'Edna' plus 'Atchison' only brings up one million obituaries."

"Ha. Speaking of Edna, we should wake Birdie. She needs to know about the teacup," Nathalie said.

"I'll give you the honors." My gaze landed on the stack

of papers on Birdie's desk. On top sat a small Ninety-Nines directory. My stomach knotted. Mom was a member. Mom was a Ninety-Nine. Maybe there was something about her inside. Curious, I flipped through the pages. I probably wouldn't even find anything. I'd take a quick peek and slip the book back under Birdie's papers and forget I even saw it. But that's the thing about having a last name that starts with the letter *A*; I was always listed first. It took two seconds to scroll down and find Penny Ashford's contact. I had done it.

I had found my mom.

And based on her mailing address, Captain Penny Ashford now lived in Hong Kong.

Oof.

I sank into Birdie's reading chair, feeling numb. No, shattered. Like someone had stomped all over my heart, then driven over it with Kate's truck. Mom got as far away from Kansas City, from us, as possible. What was wrong with, say, Milwaukee or Minnesota?

Hot tears blurred my vision. Did Dad even know where she was?

"Millie, are you okay?"

I looked up and caught Nathalie studying me.

"I'm fine," I lied.

Nathalie crossed her arms and gave me a look.

I sighed. "I found my mom's address. She's in Hong Kong. Probably with her new boyfriend."

"Ouch. I'm sorry." Nathalie gave me a hug.

I swallowed hard. "Thanks. It is what it is. I just wish she had the decency to tell me, you know? All she cares about is herself and her job." I stuffed the directory into my back pocket. "I'll bring this back. I want to jot down the address first."

"Uh, you guys?" Thea swiveled around in Birdie's chair. "Sorry to break up the sweet chitchat, but take a look at this. Birdie must have left a draft open on her desktop."

"What is it?" Cassie asked, leaning toward the screen.

"Looks like a letter," Wren said. "To the Ninety-Nines."

My heart beat fast as I skimmed the message. "This isn't a letter," I said. "This is a petition."

Dear Ninety-Nines:
The Amelia Earhart Birthplace Museum has had the distinct honor and privilege of housing the original flight goggles Amelia Earhart wore during her historic 1932 record-breaking solo transatlantic flight.

Now two worthy institutions, Purdue University and the Smithsonian National Air and Space Museum, are vying for the right to display the goggles and letter at their respective organizations. I hope you will agree with me that the best, and most appropriate, organization to house such historic items is Amelia's birthplace and museum

here in Atchison. It makes sense to keep the
collection together, and as an added bonus, their
presence drives more traffic to the museum.

   Please sign the below petition to ensure
Amelia's historic goggles and letter remain at
home in Atchison and under the care of the Ninety-
Nines, where they belong.

Sincerely,
Birdie Anderson,
Ninety-Nines member and longtime Amelia
Earhart Birthplace Museum caretaker

Robin tilted her head. "Birdie doesn't want the goggles to
leave. That's noble of her, I guess."

"Or selfish," Wren corrected in a low voice. "It also gives
her a motive for swiping them. She wants to keep the collection under her roof."

"Because if the goggles go, traffic drops, and suddenly
Birdie's out of a job," Cassie said.

Hmm. Cassie might be right.

"But Birdie's the one who got drugged. And Edna's the
one with the teacup," Thea pointed out.

I turned around, trying to process my thoughts. Did
Edna drug her boss? Did Collin? Or Perry? And who had
the goggles? None of this made sense.

Birdie snored again. She looked elegant even while sleeping. She still wore her snazzy sweater and sparkly bird earrings.

Wait a second. Birdie's left earring was missing.

I dug into my pocket for the piece of jewelry that Wren had found on the floor by the mannequins. The birds were a perfect match.

CHAPTER TWENTY-FIVE

Before I could say anything, the door to Birdie's apartment squeaked open.

Hide! Wren mouthed.

She and Nathalie squeezed into the closet. I dropped to the floor, hiding behind Birdie's bookcase. Thea dove under the desk, while Robin and Cassie ducked behind the chair in the corner.

Electra darted in, and Thea stifled a laugh. "We're afraid of a cat!"

"Not afraid. Allergic." Robin stood up and sneezed quietly. "You'll have to excuse me. I can't be around . . . Oh!" She clamped her hand over her mouth and pointed to the cat crouching in the corner. "I think we found Rosie Stancer."

I turned my head and gasped, for hanging out of Electra's mouth was Nathalie's pet rodent.

"Electra! Drop that rat. *Now*," I whispered, not wanting to wake Birdie.

Everything in the room became a blur. Nathalie rushed forward. Cassie grabbed a broom. Robin covered her eyes and rocked back and forth. "Oh my goodness, oh my goodness."

Wren reached for Birdie's wastebasket; for what, I wasn't sure.

Meanwhile, Electra watched us from the corner, as still as stone.

"That's a good kitty," Nathalie cooed, inching closer.

Electra blinked—once, twice. Her eyes shined like stars. I crouched on the floor and held out my hand. Then, without warning, Electra bolted out the door and down the stairs.

"No!" Nathalie cried, and hurried after her.

The rest of us followed, knowing full well there was no way we'd make it down the stairs and into the foyer without being seen. But that's precisely where Electra—and Rosie Stancer—went. Electra zipped down the stairs, turned around, and twitched her tail at us. I don't speak kitten, but I'd bet my Rubik's Cube Electra was gloating.

Meanwhile, I crept down the steps after Nathalie, careful to keep to the sides. If anyone stopped me, I'd say I needed a drink of water.

So far, so good.

I took another step—*creeak*—and froze.

Sweat poured down my back.

"You're doing great, Ashford," Wren whispered behind me.

I focused on my breathing. Like everything in this house, these stairs were old and creaky. At least they had carpet. I wiped my forehead and tried again.

At the halfway point, I peered into the library. Edna's back was to me. She was nestled in Birdie's chair, reading a book by the fire. Collin was there too, working a jigsaw puzzle. Like nothing horrible had transpired. But where was Chef Perry? I glanced into the huge mirror over the mantel and gasped. I was a sitting duck on the staircase. I had to hurry now. If they looked up, they would see me in the reflection.

My heart thundered as I dashed down the last two steps toward the front door.

"This way," Nathalie whispered from the entrance to the judge's parlor on my left. "Look."

I followed her into the room and stopped.

Electra was circling Birdie's coatrack. Her ears stuck straight up, on high alert.

Nathalie pleaded in a low voice, "Come on, Electra, sweetie. Be a good kitty and drop the rat."

Electra stopped circling. She looked at us, then looked at the coatrack, then back to us. I didn't move, for fear I'd spook her again.

"Nathalie, I don't think—"

"Shh. She's trying to tell us something."

I sighed. The only thing this cat wanted to tell us was how good that rat tasted.

But the cat dropped the rat. And meowed.

Rosie Stancer rolled onto her back, her pink feet stuck straight into the air.

"Oh no." I placed a hand on my friend's arm. "Is she—?"

Nathalie looked at me. "Don't be silly," she whispered. "Rosie's only pretending to be dead. She's smart like that." My friend scooped her pet into her palm and checked her over. Suddenly, Rosie leapt up and wriggled her nose. *Told you!* Natalie mouthed, and stifled a laugh. "Though she did give me a good scare."

"That's great," I whispered, "but I'm talking about the cat. Look."

Electra stood on her hind legs and frantically batted the hem of a jacket. It was dark wool and large enough for a man.

I crept closer.

"What do you want, girl?" I muttered. Electra mewed. I gave the coat a shake. Nothing fell out.

I looked at Nathalie and shrugged.

Pockets, she mouthed. Pointing to the ones on her pants. *Try. The. Pockets.*

Okay. I reached inside the left pocket and pulled out a pack of gum and a parking receipt. I squinted to make out the type.

"Purdue University! Dated last month." My heart about beat out of my chest. I flipped the coat over and reached into the right pocket. There were a couple of wadded tissues—gross—and a small wallet.

The leather was smooth black. I flipped it open and nearly died on the spot.

On one side was a bright gold badge reading: LIEUTENANT STEWART, KS POLICE, and on the other, an identification card stating: ATCHISON COUNTY POLICE, COLLIN RAY STEWART, DULY SWORN OFFICER OF ATCHISON COUNTY, KANSAS. BADGE #258.

My pulse sped up as my brain worked to connect the dots. Collin wasn't just Birdie's weird taxidermist nephew. He was a cop.

Then why had Birdie tried calling the police?

Electra meowed again. I passed the badge to Nathalie as something still rattled in that pocket. It was a bottle of vitamins. I read the label.

"Nathalie! This is valerian root."

Or, in Electra's case, catnip.

Whichever it was, Collin had used it to drug Birdie.

CHAPTER TWENTY-SIX

"Well, well. What do we have here?" Edna asked, blocking the nearest exit. Seriously? This lady appeared at the *worst* times.

Completely flustered, Nathalie fumbled Collin's badge. It hit the floor with a thud. I tried to play it cool. I even visualized a peaceful snowfall, like my school counselor taught me. Though I felt anything but cool, or peaceful.

"Oh, nothing. We were just chasing Electra. She, uh, caught a mouse." I quickly stepped on Collin's badge and hid the bottle of valerian behind my back.

Nathalie nodded innocently and shoved Rosie inside her pocket. "A real mouse. Whiskers and everything."

Edna cocked her head and gave us a funny look. "Well, good for Electra. But I think it's past lights-out. You two should zip upstairs, and—"

"Hold it." Collin strolled into the parlor. He was still carrying his taxidermy textbook, though I hadn't seen him read past the first few pages. "Someone's been doing some snooping when they should have been snoozing."

My cheeks flushed. This night was quickly spiraling into a nightmare. I wanted to call my dad. Now. But I couldn't let Collin know I was crumbling inside. I couldn't let him bully us. "Why didn't you tell us you were a cop?"

Collin sighed. "It's complicated. And none of your business."

"Complicated," I said. "*That* I'll buy. But this *is* our business. You wait until we talk to the Ninety-Nines and police about our sleepover. *Oh, it was really fun, right up until one of the grown-ups, you know, drugged the docent.*" To drive the point home, I rattled the bottle of valerian capsules in his face.

Edna gasped and immediately moved herself between us and him. "Stewart, you have some explaining to do."

Stewart! So that's who Edna was talking to.

"And you!" I said, pointing to Edna. "You're not who you pretend to be either. We saw you stealing the evidence."

Collin faced Edna. "Theft and tampering; those are strong accusations. You'd better start talking, Officer."

Officer! My jaw hit the floor.

"I so did not see that coming," said Nathalie.

"That's enough!" Edna drew her fingers across her

mouth in the universal sign for *zip it.* "Not stealing. Securing. I was securing the evidence, so the lab could dust for fingerprints."

"Aha. Dusting you actually can do," I said. Nathalie's eyes grew huge, but I was on a roll and couldn't shut up. "This explains so much."

The others came booming down the stairs. "What's going on?" asked Wren.

I drew a shaky breath. "Collin drugged Birdie, and he and Edna are both cops."

"Surprise." Edna smirked.

"Wait. What?" asked Thea.

Wren crossed her arms. "I feel so much safer."

"Stop, all of you." An exasperated Collin waved his hands as he spoke. "I didn't drug anyone. I take valerian to help me sleep because of my shoulder. When Birdie asked me to set humane rodent traps, I knew the valerian would lure the rats inside without killing them. So, yes, the valerian root is mine, but no, I didn't give it to my aunt." He took a big breath. "And I really am a cop."

"And I'm the tooth fairy," said Wren.

"He's telling the truth, Wren." I tossed her his badge.

Collin looked annoyed but relieved. "Listen, my aunt doesn't know I'm a cop. She believes I'm a rising star in the world of taxidermy. I am, but it's all because I work undercover. This"—he gestured to his boots and flannel—"is a persona. I learned taxidermy to help the game warden nab wildlife poachers and code violators."

Wren handed him his badge. "So, you're either a good cop or an even better liar."

"Yes."

"Then explain this Purdue parking pass. We all know they wanted the goggles too." I waved the slip in front of his face. Behind me, Cassie gasped.

Collin put up his hands. "So now I'm being interrogated? I went to a game with friends! You can verify with them. I'm not the bad guy here, Detective."

Adrenaline pumped through my veins. Detective! Ha. Those were fighting words. "Then why was your scalpel pinned to the mannequin?"

Collin shook his head. "I don't know. I don't know! Edna and I searched every nook and cranny for those goggles. My job was to protect them, and I failed." He stared at the ceiling. "I haven't even told my boss, as I'd hoped to recover them first. As for the scalpel, I must have dropped it somewhere. Or someone took it."

Edna unwrapped a peppermint. "We owe it to you girls to know the truth. Birdie hired me three weeks ago. She worried someone would try to steal the goggles thanks to the amazing press they've recently received. Obviously, Collin and I couldn't let on that we knew each other." She calmly popped the candy into her mouth.

"Okay. But what about Chef Perry? He was a new hire too," I said.

Edna looked at Collin. "We didn't have anything to do with that. That was all the Ninety-Nines looking after Birdie. Now, if you will please leave the detecting to—"

Birdie. I'd almost forgotten. I reached into my pocket and pulled out her earring.

"That's Birdie's," Edna snapped. "What are you doing with it?"

"Wren found it on the floor, by the goggles display," I replied.

"Yup. I saw the whole thing," said Robin.

"That doesn't mean anything," Collin said. "That earring could have fallen off at any time." Turning to Edna, he asked, "Are we really going to let some kids outdetect us?"

Edna held out her hand. "I'll take that, thank you very much. Now, as I was saying a moment ago, if you girls can please leave the detecting to us, we will make sure everyone stays safe."

Robin looked over her glasses.

"Safe, like that time when a mannequin with a threatening letter stabbed to its chest fell out of the wardrobe and onto my friend?" asked Thea.

"Or safe, as in spending twenty-four hours snowed in with a crook?" Cassie added. "There are so many instances of 'safe,' someone will be hearing from my lawyer."

I found my cube. The familiar clicks and clacks were rhythmic and soothing. Unlike this conversation.

"Ooh. I know! How about that time Birdie—oh, what do you call it—collapsed? Or when Collin *hid inside* Amelia's bedroom closet?" Nathalie continued, practically yelling. She was obviously still steamed about the rattraps and, well, everything else. Crumb, we all were.

I must have appeared calm, quietly cubing, while everyone's emotions swirled like the blowing snow outside. But beneath the surface, my brain buzzed. Just because an earring was dropped near the crime scene didn't make someone a crook. Nor did owning a scalpel. Or a bottle of herbs. But together, these items told a story. If only I knew how it ended.

The list of clues felt like a monster jigsaw puzzle with only the edges complete. I had to fill in the pieces.

Then Nathalie broke down in tears. I felt like doing the same myself, to be honest.

"Things will be okay, Nathalie," I said, even though I had no guarantees they would be. "We have to believe everything will work out."

Thea marched over. "Hey, Nat, forget Collin. When you talk to friends back home, what are you going to say you saw in Amelia's closet?"

Nathalie wiped her eyes. "This sounds like the start of a really bad joke."

Thea laughed. "Maybe so. But think about it. How many people get to visit Amelia Earhart's childhood room and peek inside her closet? We did that. *We* know what's stored there."

"Yeah." Natalie grunted. "Dusty holiday decor."

Thea grinned. "Exactly. There could have been anything in there. Anything. Even the goggles. We were so excited! Then Millie opened the door and found—wait for it—a few wreaths, some old ornaments, and—"

"A faux tree." Nathalie started to laugh.

Thea giggled. "A fake tree! Now *that's* funny. In Amelia Earhart's closet. Who'd have thought?"

I smiled. A Christmas tree wouldn't be my first guess either, though obviously some people loved them. . . . *Oh my goggles.*

My heart stopped. "Say that again, Thea."

Thea looked at me like I'd lost my marbles. "We searched Amelia's closet and found holiday decorations? You saw the extra wreaths, ornaments, and an old tree. It was like Santa's workshop in there."

"That's it. That's it!" I whirled around and marched out of the room.

"Hey! No one is going anywhere," Collin yelled after me. "Give it up, Millie. We're the professionals here."

But it was too late. I had already made my way across the foyer and into the library, where I gazed up at Birdie's dazzling Christmas tree. The tree she'd painstakingly decked out in red bows, glittering airplanes, and all things aviation. The tree she'd fastidiously fussed over like a nervous parent. It took me a minute to find the right pair among the two dozen replicas, but I'd seen the tape across the lenses before.

"Super professional," I said, and whipped around, holding Amelia Earhart's goggles.

CHAPTER TWENTY-SEVEN

"Oh my goodness, oh my goodness," Robin cried.

"How on earth did they get there?" Collin sputtered.

"You tell me, Collin." My whole body vibrated with nerves and the thrill of finding the prize.

His face turned as red as Amelia's plane. "For the last time, I don't know. There are so many goggles in this darn house, I can't keep track."

Thea tightened her strap. "You can say that again."

Edna popped her second peppermint and smiled. I wondered how many cavities she'd had. "All that matters is we have them now, thank God, and can keep them in good condition. Hand them over, Millie. We'll make sure they get to Washington as planned."

I looked at the cracked leather strap, the scratched lenses.

So much history in one small package. I moved to hand them over, but my heart kicked with resistance. Suddenly, a furious fire ignited inside me. A flame so hot I couldn't ignore it.

"Don't you want to know who swiped them?" I asked. "Who drugged Birdie? Who threatened us?" I motioned to the others. "Don't you care about justice and loyalty and fierce independence? Because Amelia did. She stood up not just for women but for all kinds of people. She stood up and spoke up for what was right."

Edna's face softened. "Of course I do. I want all of that, Millie, for Birdie and for you. You and your friends deserve answers, too." She sighed and studied the ceiling. "Listen. Do you know how hard it is to be a female police officer?"

I shook my head. No, I didn't know. But mom caught flak for having a career as a pilot.

"Pretty darn difficult," Edna snapped. "We work hard to be taken seriously." She stopped and rubbed her temples. Her navy nail polish was badly chipped. Something told me Edna's prickliness was more than annoyance at us.

"What I mean is, we women need to stick together. I'm on your side, Millie. Birdie wouldn't have reached out to me had she not been concerned, all right? I'm proud of you. *You* did this"—she pointed to the goggles in my hand—"all of you. You recovered Amelia Earhart's goggles. But I need to ask for them, to finish *my* job."

I looked at the flimsy goggles, then over at my friends.

Thea shrugged. Nathalie nodded. Why was life so confusing and complex?

Edna held out her hand. "I know I come across as gruff, but you can trust me, Millie. I promise."

Reluctantly, I let go of Amelia's goggles.

Then the whole house went dark.

"Again? *That's* not creepy," cried Nathalie.

"I told you this house was haunted," said Thea. "Somebody better phone Amelia and say we found her goggles."

Gusts of wind whistled through the eaves, shaking windows and rattling doors.

"The sooner the better," said Nathalie.

Somewhere in the house a door slammed. I bet every one of us jumped.

Edna coughed. "Perry must have finished in the kitchen."

"At least the neighbors have power. They must use a timer like we do when we're away," Robin mused. "I love white Christmas lights." Robin found beauty in everything. It was her superpower. The world could be ending, and she'd be thrilled we stayed for the credits. I should be more like Robin.

Collin grunted and struck a match. "I guess it's time to flip the breaker again." He lit the nearest candle. The flame was hauntingly beautiful in the dark.

"I'll go," Thea volunteered. "Where's the switch?"

Collin ran a hand over his beard. "The cellar."

✳ ✳ ✳

I shuddered. The cellar. Of course.

The place where rats live and thrive. Immediately, my pulse sped up, and I began to sweat.

"Oh, heck no." Thea put up her hands. "You know there are ghosts down there."

"And rats. And spiders." Robin pushed her glasses onto her nose.

"Don't forget a low probability of murder," I added.

Thea shot me a nasty look. I shrugged. "Math."

Nathalie said, "Why don't we all go down together?"

It's not every day the opportunity to tour Amelia Earhart's cellar presents itself, and we wanted to be wise about it. Still, I died a thousand deaths descending those stairs.

"The breaker box is at the bottom of the steps, to the left," Collin called down after us. "There should be extra candles in a box beneath it. There's a light bulb overhead."

"Got it," said Thea. She'd been the first to go, the brave one holding the flashlight.

Unsurprisingly, the Otises' basement was cold, damp, and dark. But thanks to a row of high windows, streams of moonlight pierced the dark. Until the clouds shifted. Then what little light we had winked out.

"I got you," said Robin. A small beam of light clicked on.

"Wait. Where'd you get a flashlight?" asked Wren.

Robin grinned. "I took advantage of the power outage and snagged your phone from the basket."

"You what?" Wren hugged her sister. "You're brilliant! Of course, you *are* related to me."

Robin shrugged. "Thanks. I thought I was getting *my* phone, but, well, it was dark, and—"

"Wait a second. Birdie locked that cabinet," interrupted Nathalie. "How did you get in?"

"Oh, that!" Robin laughed. "Minor detail. Remember in Birdie's apartment, when we were trying to guess her password?"

"Yes. Get on with it," said Wren.

"Well, I had been looking at the model plane on her nightstand when Birdie made that sound, almost like a wheeze. I froze, but she rolled over, and this tiny key was lying on the sheet. I figured it fell from her pocket. So, I borrowed it! See?"

Robin shook the shiny key from her boot.

"Amazing," said Wren.

"I was hoping it went to the phone cabinet, and it did!" Robin beamed. "But there's still no service, and your battery's showing twenty percent."

"We'll conserve it," I said. "Quick thinking, Robin." I wished she'd grabbed my phone, but one device was better than none.

"And if the power comes back, we can charge it," said Cassie.

"We can charge all our phones. Okay, shine that light over here," said Thea.

Thea located the electric panel easily enough. The first order of business was to make sure there was no standing water nearby. Then, holding her flashlight between her teeth, she worked her way down two vertical columns of circuit breakers, flipping each switch one by one. Once these switches were in the "off" position, she located the main breaker. "That's funny. It's already off. Hmm; cross your fingers this does the trick." *Click.* "Now, to reset each circuit."

We waited while she toggled each switch one at a time. At last we heard a fan clink to life.

"Hooray!" I cheered.

"You're a wizard, Thea." Wren waved a pretend wand in the air. "Let's rescue the rest of our devices and find some snacks."

Thea closed the small metal door and laughed. "You don't have to ask me twice." But when we reached the door at the top of the steps, Thea stopped short. "No, no, no."

"Thea, what's wrong?" I asked.

She jiggled the handle, frantic. "It's locked. It's locked!"

Dread filled my stomach. How could we have been so stupid?

"Hey! HEY!" Thea shouted, then pounded her palm against the wood. "The dead bolt's thrown. You can see it through the crack."

Panic rose in my throat. It was cold down here. We had no water, no food, no cell signal. No way to communicate with the outside world. "Edna! Collin! Perry! This isn't funny, guys. Let us out!" I rattled the door handle.

Meanwhile, Nathalie wriggled underneath me and studied the latch. "Yeah, there's no way to pick that. But the good news is, our parents will be here tomorrow. If the roads clear."

"I am not spending the night in this cellar, no thank you," said Robin.

"Oh, come on. Think of all the poetry it will inspire!" Wren knocked down a cobweb.

"This isn't time for jokes, Wren. We don't know what they have planned," I said. "They could poison us, or chop us up into bits and boil us, or—"

"Millie. Stop." Wren placed her hand, and bit of cobweb, on my shoulder. "We're getting out of this, together. That's our only option."

I swallowed and brushed the cobweb away. "Right. Sorry. I default to thinking up worst-case scenarios."

"Let's fixate on helpful ones instead. Like how we're going to escape," said Cassie.

I thought for a moment. "We could hack our way out."

"Brilliant!" Cassie said. "If only we had an ax."

I searched the cellar for one while the others took turns pounding on the door. After a few moments, I found a useless spade, and Wren's voice had turned hoarse from shouting.

"Hey! HEY! Let us out, you big bunch of jerks!"

"Save your energy," said Robin. "They aren't coming."

With a final kick, I collapsed on the stairs, exhausted and angry.

"I can't believe I trusted them," I said.

"Don't beat yourself up. It's not your fault they have the goggles." Sitting crisscross, Cassie cradled her chin in her hand and sighed.

"Yeah, the way Edna gave that whole emotional speech, just so you'd hand the goggles over. That was gross," said Nathalie.

"So gross." Thea clicked her flashlight off and back on.

"But I didn't," I said.

Thea turned the flashlight on me. "Didn't what?"

"Huh?" Cassie sat up. "I watched you."

"What are you saying, Ashford?" asked Wren.

I couldn't hide my smile any longer. "I gave them replicas."

CHAPTER TWENTY-EIGHT

Nathalie laughed. "You did not!"

I nodded, feeling a little smug. "I didn't think those two would know the difference, and, well, Birdie's still sleeping."

"Snooze City," said Nathalie.

Robin's shoulders drooped. "I guess this means you didn't find the real goggles, then."

"Oh no, they were there, all right. See?" For once I had something besides my Rubik's Cube stashed in my hoodie pocket. I held up a delicate strip of leather attached to aluminum frames.

"Get out!" Wren slugged me in the arm. "These are Amelia's goggles?"

"Holy moly," Thea whispered. "Check out the fabric adhesive on the lenses."

"Tape. To reduce the sun's glare over the Atlantic," said Nathalie. "Pretty smart, huh?"

"The glass is even tinted orange," said Cassie. "Amber lenses are helpful in low-light conditions, as they make the surroundings appear brighter."

"This is amazing!" said Robin, holding out her hand. "May I?"

"Sure." I placed the artifact in her palm.

Wren shook her head in awe. "Unbelievable! But how did you know they'd be in the tree?"

I tucked a piece of hair behind my ear, secretly pleased with myself. "I didn't. But when Thea mentioned finding a Christmas tree in the closet upstairs, I remembered Birdie fussing over the one in the library after dinner. That, combined with the earring you found near the case—it was just a hunch."

"Let me get this straight. You think Birdie stole the goggles from herself?" asked Robin.

I shook my head. "Not from herself. From the Ninety-Nines—well, the Smithsonian. They're supposed to pick them up in two days. Remember the letter Thea found on Birdie's computer? It all makes sense."

"Oh yeah," said Robin. "She wanted to keep the goggles here, with Amelia's things."

"What she wanted to keep is her job," added Cassie.

"That too. Wait a minute. If Birdie swiped the goggles,

who drugged her?" Nathalie asked as Rosie explored nearby. "Ow. This hurts my head."

I rubbed my temples. "Yours and mine both."

Robin gave me the goggles. "So, what are you going to do with them?"

I stopped. Robin's comment caught me by surprise. "I didn't really think about that part. They should go to the police. But what do I do with them now?"

"You could stash them somewhere down here," suggested Thea.

"Too risky," said Cassie. "The cellar's not climate controlled. The lenses and leather would be exposed to a range of temperatures or, worse, rodents."

"She's not wrong," said Nathalie. "Maybe hide them in your hoodie like before and smuggle them out. You fooled all of us."

I nodded, suddenly feeling a little nauseated. If I tripped and smashed Amelia Earhart's lenses . . . Well, I wouldn't. That's all there was to that. The alternative was too awful to imagine. Even so, I wanted to barf.

"Speaking of fooling people, we need to get out of here before the grown-ups figure out the swap." Wren hopped up and dusted off her hands. "Hey, Thea?"

Thea's eyebrows arched. "Yeah?"

"Can you drive your aunt's bike?"

Thea balked. "Can I drive my auntie's bike? Can I, Thea

Cooke, drive my auntie's bike? Girlfriend, I *built* my auntie's bike."

"Great!" Wren clapped Thea on the back. "Because you're about to drive the two of us into town."

"Whoa. Whoa. And whoa." Robin poked her sister in the chest. "Don't you get any wild ideas. You think you're bad to the bone, but you aren't equipped to survive a blizzard. On a *bike*! There's a reason Thea's aunt got a ride to the hotel. Plus, the engine starting would give us away!"

Wren grabbed her sister's shoulders. "We're from Minne-*snow*-ta, remember?"

Robin rolled her eyes. "I don't care, Wren. This isn't a time to be funny. This is dangerous."

"And staying here isn't?" Cassie added. "Let's face it. They've left us down here to rot."

"Maybe they did, but we don't have time for a pity party. We need every one of our smarts to survive." Thea turned the flashlight around. "Is there any grown-up we can trust?"

Nathalie coaxed Rosie to the steps. "I don't know. Edna and Collin already tricked us by pretending to be something they're not. Which wasn't terrible until he locked us in the dungeon."

I wandered over to a worktable shoved against the wall. Tiny jars of metallic paint, tubes of cement, and miniature airplane parts littered the surface. A wheel here, a propeller there. Sticker sheets with faded decals. I picked up the blue paint and unscrewed the lid. Dry as a bone. At one time, somebody sat here and built model planes. "And Collin doesn't care about his aunt, past using her. Birdie said he rarely visits, and when he does, he hogs her computer and eats all her food."

"Yeah. Do you think he drugged her?" asked Robin.

I turned and shrugged. "It's possible, especially if he locked us down here. But I don't see a clear motive. If Collin's telling the truth about working with the game warden, why would he drug Birdie? Was he after the goggles? And why now? He's been around them for years. Not to mention, he seems pretty content in general. The man lives with his parents."

"So, he wants money for his own place," said Robin. "Or he wants to impress Edna."

"Ew. Maybe." I scratched my head.

"Okay, say someone framed him," said Cassie. "Who would have known Collin was trapping rodents? Maybe they swiped a few of his valerian capsules and added them to her tea."

"But why go to that much trouble to frame someone?" Nathalie asked. "And leave the warning note, too?"

Wren sighed. "Would Edna? Maybe she has some horrible vendetta against Birdie. Or she held something against Collin at work."

"Perhaps," said Thea. "Don't forget the crushed peppermint we found. Edna's always eating them."

"Mint helps with nausea," added Cassie. "Maybe she has an upset stomach."

"Or maybe she just likes them," said Thea.

I picked up the finished models one by one and blew off decades of dust. There was a World War II plane, a blue Travel Air stamped with Louise Thaden's signature, and two of Amelia's planes—the *Friendship* and her red Lockheed Vega. But the next plane grabbed me and wouldn't let go.

"Perry." I turned the plane over in my hand.

"What?" asked Robin.

"Perry asked Collin for traps, remember? He said he saw rat droppings in the kitchen. What if he made it all up?"

Cassie tilted her head. "So, instead of setting traps, Perry took the valerian from them to drug Birdie. Holy fib!"

"There's also this." I showed them the replica plane.

Thea gasped. "Oh. My grandfather has that model. It's an Avro Avian flown by some Australian pilot."

"First solo flight from England to Australia," added Wren. "We did a crash course on Australian aviation history on our channel."

"Well, whoever it belongs to, it's an exact match to Perry's tattoo," I said.

"Are you sure about that?" Thea looked at me.

"Positive. This model has a registration of G-EBOV. The same sequence on Perry's arm. We know from the photograph upstairs that Amelia's Avro Avian was marked

G-EBUG. Close, but no champagne. Either Perry tatted the wrong plane on purpose, for some reason unknown to us, or he's not the Amelia buff he claims to be."

"Which means he probably lied about other stuff, too. Like working at the White House!" said Nathalie.

"Probably." I looked at my friends. "But what's his motive?"

Robin closed her eyes. "Let's see; didn't Birdie say something at dinner about a culinary school? That's got to be expensive."

I nodded. "We need the police."

"If only we had cell service." Robin sighed.

"You girls may be from the land of snow and ice, but I'm from the state of Texas. We have cattle, queso, and parkas for anytime the temp falls below seventy-two." Thea paused for a hot second. Maybe she was dreaming of chips and salsa. "We could go on foot, but we'll need coats."

"Count me in. But first we have to bust out," said Wren.

I pulled my ponytail tighter and scanned the room. "Those windows are awfully high."

Cassie kicked some dirt around. "We could slide a note under the door. Say Robin needs her medicine . . ."

Wren's eyes lit up. "And when they open the door, we jump them!"

I winced.

"That's not *exactly* what I had in mind." Cassie blew on

her fingers to warm them. "I think the windows are our best bet for staying undetected."

"Agreed," said Wren. "Though I can't promise I won't kick some shins if I get the chance."

"Oh my goodness." Robin wrapped her arms around her middle. Her eyes were puffy from allergies. "Does it have to be so dark and dank down here? There's probably mold, too. Do you think there's mold?"

"It *is* a cellar. It's supposed to be dark, and of course there's mold." Wren tugged on a chain dangling from the ceiling. A light buzzed, like it was trying to wake up. She jumped back, startled by a clothed mannequin in the corner. "These mannequins keep giving me heart attacks. This one's in full Amelia flight gear, though. Check out her cap, jacket, and boots."

"They do love their creepy mannequin theme," Robin said, then sneezed. "It helps to name them. She looks like an Agnes."

Nathalie rubbed grime off the mannequin's face. "Hi, Agnes. I hope we're not down here as long as you."

I shoved aside an old crate of mason jars, candles, and rope to reach one of twenty boxes stacked in the corner. "No kidding. Agnes has been busy guarding Beech-Nut brand tomato juice. Cases and cases of tomato juice."

"Look on the bright side," Nathalie said. "We won't starve."

"If only we had a way to open them," I said.

Thea grunted. "All we need is an ice pick. Amelia always flew with one. Not for emergencies, but to open her many cans of juice."

I smacked my forehead. "That's right! She had an endorsement deal with Beech-Nut. Her family probably got free tomato juice for years."

"If the cans are that old, then they probably contain botulism, too." Nathalie shuddered. "No thank you. I don't want any part of scary toxins."

Cassie slid one of the boxes across the dirt floor, stopping underneath a high window. "Me neither. Care to help?"

"Sure." I shoved another box next to the first. "Based on the layout of the house, this window should face north onto Santa Fe Street."

Wren pushed another case over. Then another. We began stacking them. We were playing Tetris, that old video game my dad loved. With tomato juice.

"One more should do it," I said.

"There are no more boxes," Wren called. "Just cans of paint, the mannequin, and this old beast, buried behind the juice." She flopped a suitcase down in front of us.

It was old luggage, all right. Old, broken in, brown. The hard-shell kind, covered in leather and impervious to dents. I used my sleeve to brush away a layer of dust.

The seams were carefully stitched. The handle still

wiggled back and forth. And a silver nameplate by the grip was engraved with the owner's name.

I tilted the suitcase so the metal plate reflected in the moonlight. Time froze.

"Uh. You guys." I rubbed my eyes to make sure I wasn't imagining things. "Are you seeing what I'm seeing?"

Wren read over my shoulder. "*A. M. E.*"

"Right," I said. "Amelia Mary—"

"Earhart." Wren's eyes grew wide. "Well, don't just sit there. Open it!"

I tried both latches. "Drat. It's locked tight."

"Let me try." Wren wriggled her way to the front. "Ugh. Millie's right."

"There has to be a way in without damaging it," Robin said.

"I got it," Nathalie said. She reached up and pulled out a hairpin that was holding her braid.

I looked from Wren to the others, my mouth agape. Who knew Nathalie could pick locks? Thea looked at me and shrugged.

"Give her some space," Cassie bossed. "A girl needs room to work."

Nathalie kneeled on the ground in front of the case. After inspecting the type of lock, she positioned the suitcase so it stood upright. She inserted the pin into the first lock, the one on the left, and bent her ear closer to the latch as she worked. None of us dared to make a sound. A strand of hair fell in front of her face and she blew it away. It might be dark in the basement, but I still caught the lines of concentration on her forehead in the moonlight.

She shook her head in frustration. "Older locks tend to stick. And if this one really is Amelia's . . ."

"It could be a century old," Cassie whispered.

Wren whistled. "Are you guys thinking what I'm thinking?"

"That we have a legit time capsule on our hands?" said Thea.

Nathalie looked up. "It could be a movie prop. Birdie said there are plenty of those around."

My heart raced, and I looked from face to face to face. Ten hours ago we were complete strangers, and now, by some strange twist of fate, they had become my friends.

"Where did you learn to pick locks?" I asked.

Nathalie smirked. "In the summers, I'd go to work with my mom in the lab. She'd let me play with a few rats, if I could get them out without using a key. That's how I got to keep Rosie. Anyway, it's not that difficult once you know how."

I smiled. Cubing was the same. There were basic principles to master, which of course seemed daunting to everyone else.

"Bingo." Nathalie smiled as the left lock flipped back.

Robin and Cassie cheered.

The energy in the room was electric. I could almost imagine Amelia with us, nodding along her encouragement.

Nathalie worked for a few seconds longer before the right latch sprang open as well.

"You are a mad genius." Wren smacked her on the back.

"Well, the one side was a little sticky." Nathalie smiled and pushed the pin back into her hair. "But thanks."

We stared at the case. No one wanted to be the first to break the spell. What if the suitcase was filled with rocks?

But what if it wasn't?

CHAPTER TWENTY-NINE

"Now for the big reveal!" Cassie clapped.

Wren scratched her nose. "Hold on. I think Nathalie should have the honors of lifting the lid. She picked the locks."

"And I think Millie should be the one to open it. She's the one who found it."

I put my hand on the smooth leather and looked at Nathalie. "Let's go together. On the count of three."

Nathalie nodded.

"One," Wren counted. "Robin, make sure to document this."

"Already on it," she replied, holding up Wren's phone.

Butterflies tumbled in my stomach.

"Two."

My lips twitched.

"Three!"

The lid sprang open. We stepped back.

The suitcase appeared to be neatly packed, as if for a trip.

"Look! Jodhpurs," Cassie said.

I reached inside and carefully picked up the pants, afraid they'd disintegrate. But the cool air in the cellar must have helped to preserve them over time. They fell open with a swish and looked like blousy slacks that grew tight below the knee.

"Those might be the ugliest pants I've ever seen." Wren wrinkled her nose. "Do you think Amelia actually wore them?"

"For sure. She helped make pants trendy for women," said Nathalie.

"What else is in there?" Cassie peered over my shoulder.

"Oh wow. A full flight suit!" I ran my fingers over the hand-sewn aviator patches. My fingers tingled, and I felt a little breathless. Amelia was a skilled seamstress, with her own clothing line. She most likely sewed these badges on herself. I couldn't believe our luck. "Feel how soft the inside is. Insulated and lined in flannel."

Cassie picked up the garment. "The flannel is for warmth. Imagine being in an open-cockpit plane. Brrr!"

"What's that?" Nathalie pointed to a small red bag. I picked it up, and the contents made a familiar *clack*. I looked inside and laughed. "Marbles."

"Maybe they were for her stepson." Cassie inspected a yellow one and dropped it back with a *clunk*.

"This is better than all the holidays combined," Robin gasped, and put away the phone.

"Look, there are leather gloves and a coordinating scarf, and oh!" My heart stopped. The last item in Amelia Earhart's suitcase looked fragile.

"Please don't tell me you've found Amelia Earhart's underwear."

"No." I shot Wren a look. "She flew in men's boxers. But this is better." I held up a small green jar.

Cassie took the glass container and unscrewed the lid. "Whoa, get a whiff of that."

"Smelling salts!" Wren said with a laugh. "Pilots used them on long flights to stay awake."

On cue, the wind shrieked.

"They're going to leave us down here until morning, aren't they?" Robin's voice quivered.

"Not if I can help it." Thea climbed up the mountain of boxes. She pressed her nose to the narrow window. "Show-and-tell was nice and all, but if we're going to get help, we need to move. *Now*." She unlocked the window and turned back around to face us. "Who's with me?"

Cassie gasped. "You can't go outside like that. You'll freeze!"

"Cassie's right, Thea. What's your plan?" I looked at my friend.

"We'll sneak out to the side street. Run to one of the neighbors, in case Birdie's wrong and someone's home. If that doesn't work, it's a short trek to the police station downtown."

"What about coats?" Nathalie asked.

Thea pointed to the luggage. "Between the suitcase and Agnes, we have all the necessary warm accessories."

Wren marched over to the mannequin and unwound her scarf. "Sorry, Agnes. I need to borrow this. And this."

"Wren? What are you doing?" her sister asked.

Wren stepped inside the old flight suit. It was a perfect fit. "Going with Thea. No one's flying solo tonight."

CHAPTER THIRTY

"Wren, wait." Cassie put out her hand. "Let me go. You can stay here with Robin."

She motioned to Robin, who wiped away a tear. I couldn't tell whether it was from allergies or worry about Wren leaving.

But Wren had made up her mind, and we all knew there was no use in arguing with her.

Nathalie coughed. "It's five blocks to the police department. We passed it, the fire department, and the library on the way in."

The girls dressed in nervous silence. "How do we look?" asked Thea, tugging her flight cap over her ears.

"Amazing," said Nathalie.

"Like real aviatrixes," I said.

"Cool," Wren said. "Hey, Robin, take our picture. It's not

every day you wear Amelia Earhart's flight gear. Let's just hope the threads hold up, huh, Thea?"

Cassie brushed a piece of fuzz, or maybe a spider, off Thea's shoulder. "You'll have the cold on your side for that. Say 'cheese'!"

"Cheese."

Click.

I smiled. Wren lived for marketable moments like this. Hashtag adventure.

Next to me, Robin sniffled.

"Okay." Wren's brow creased as she looked from Cassie and me to her sister. "What's your plan after we leave?"

"Operation Hold Out until Help Arrives." I pinched my lips together to hide my worried smile. "No pressure."

"Very funny," Wren said. "You still need a plan of attack."

I looked down at my cube, and a zany idea popped into my head. "Have you ever seen *Home Alone*?"

A slow grin crept across Wren's face. "Ashford, I like the way you think."

"Millie, one more thing." Thea undid one of her friendship bracelets and tied it to my wrist. "For good luck."

My throat grew tight. Amelia wore a lucky bracelet. Now I did too. "Thanks. What about you two?" I asked. "You're the ones going out into the snow."

"We'll stick to the streets."

I studied the multicolored threads on my wrist. "You'd

better come back, Thea Cooke. You owe me a bike ride."

Thea tugged her flight cap down around her ears and buckled the chin strap. "You got it. Wren, you ready?"

"Always." Wren gave her sister a quick hug. "Now, remember, shoot all video in landscape mode, and whatever you do, hold still!"

Robin nodded and cleaned the lens on Wren's phone. "Hold still. Okay. Be careful, Wren."

"Don't drop my phone."

On top of the boxes, Thea struggled with the window. It was frozen and probably hadn't been opened since the Clinton administration, but she raised it just enough to slip through. A blast of cold air shot into the cellar, and she wriggled her way outside. Wren made a peace sign then slid out after her. The last thing we saw was the sheen of her moon boots.

I scrambled up the crates and lowered the window to keep out the cold. I didn't latch it. If they needed a way back in, I wanted them to have one.

"Now what?" Nathalie asked.

Hopping down, I channeled my inner boss. We didn't have time to despair. We had to act now, before we chickened out. "We can't let them win; we have to work fast. Robin?"

Robin dried her eyes and looked at me.

"Grab the rope and tie it around the mannequin's middle. I want her hoisted as high above the stairs as possible."

"Got it."

"Nathalie and Cassie, I need your help over here. Amelia wouldn't sit around waiting to be rescued, and we're not going to either."

Robin threw the end of the rope over some ductwork and hoisted a flying—and now naked—Agnes to the ceiling. The mannequin floated high above our heads like Supergirl. Nathalie and I built a tin can pyramid beneath her, about two feet from the bottom step. The pyramid was every bit as tall as we were and decidedly epic. Cassie put the crowning can on top, while Robin held the end of Agnes's rope in her hands and waited. As long as the rope remained taut, Agnes stayed in place.

I needed her to fly a bit longer.

Nathalie and I positioned Amelia's marbles up and down the steps, and Cassie killed the light.

We'd no sooner finished when the door squeaked.

A flashlight beam swept across the basement, blinding us down in the dark. I shielded my eyes and squinted.

"Having fun yet?" Collin's voice boomed from the doorway. His boots fell heavy—*clomp, clomp*—on the creaky stairs. Cool air hit the back of my neck, and my heart hammered. *Please, let this work.*

"Sorry about the lock. Sometimes the door swings shut so hard it falls into place. At any rate, we don't have much time." He looked over his shoulder, then back to us. "Play along with me," he whispered.

What? I looked to Nathalie. She bit her nails.

"You must be thirsty. I've brought drinks." He yanked one of his earbuds out. Oh. Was that why he hadn't heard us?

My teeth began to chatter. My breath grew short. He must be bonkers to think we'd drink anything prepared by adults in this house. I tried to speak, but my voice had checked out. I needed my cube. No. No, I didn't.

I needed my family.

My dad. I needed my dad. Dad would know what to do. And I was going to do everything in my power to make sure I saw him again.

"Actually, Collin." I coughed to hide the tremble in my voice. "A drink of water would be nice."

Nathalie dug her nails into me as Collin swung his flashlight around to find us in the dark. "Hold on. There's only four of you." He reached for a radio on his hip.

My blood became ice as Collin's flashlight bobbed from Nathalie to Cassie to Robin and then back to me again.

I couldn't breathe. This was it. Game. Over.

Collin crept closer. Light streamed in from the hallway, illuminating his lanky silhouette.

"I'm not going to hurt you. I just need to know where your friends went."

I shook my head. Friends don't betray friends.

Collin sighed and raised the radio to his mouth. "Four-eleven to Dispatch. Four-eleven to Dispatch. Come in, Dispatch. Over." The radio crackled in response.

Of course. A radio could call for help. A radio could contact the police, or fire department, or nearby truckers. Like Kate.

Or a radio could chat with your cronies upstairs.

"Wait!" I yelled. But I was too late.

Collin stepped onto the marbles. His arms windmilled, and I winced as the radio sailed through the air. His feet flew out from under him. And down he went.

Collin's head smacked against the wooden stairs once, twice, while his feet careened into the mound of cans. The tower of juice toppled, and Robin released the rope. Like clockwork, Agnes dropped from the sky, crashing on top of him. Collin moaned but didn't move. He couldn't.

Collin was trapped.

CHAPTER THIRTY-ONE

Crumb. The radio was smashed to bits.

"Millie, come on!" Cassie tugged at my arm.

Breathless, we bolted upstairs. With a quick flick of my wrist I locked Collin in the basement.

"It actually worked!" I whispered, and gave Nathalie a high five. But there was one thing we hadn't thought of. What came next.

Cassie held a finger to her lips. Perry and Edna lurked in the house, and here we stood, exposed. We had to think fast. The entrance to the basement, where we were now, was located underneath the grand staircase in the foyer, the space where the butler's pantry, library, and gift shop came together. We couldn't stay here in the open. We had to pick a room.

Perry was probably in the kitchen, so the gift shop was out. The library held our remaining phones—our best chance at contacting help—plus it was near the front door. But even that was risky. Edna was always by the fire. Cassie nodded toward the butler's pantry, and she had a valid point. If we could make it through the pantry and into the breezeway, we could exit out the side door.

Anything sounded safer than staying inside this house.

All was quiet. Eerily quiet. We had to move. Now.

I looked from Cassie to Robin to Nathalie and pointed to the door. They nodded in unison.

Nathalie whispered, "One.

"Two.

"Three!" And took off.

She poked her head around the door frame and waved for us to follow.

Robin ran, then Cassie.

I started to go but stopped. I heard a faint cry. It sounded like a cat, or maybe a small child.

The sound happened again, and I was sure it came from the library. Curiosity pulled me down the hall, even though the other way, the way of my friends, screamed freedom.

"Millie!" Nathalie whispered.

I froze, stuck in a mental game of tug-of-war. *What would Amelia do?* I knew what *this* Amelia would do: She'd dart out the nearest door, anxious and afraid, thinking only of herself.

But that was before—before she'd met new friends, explored a secret passage, and trapped a man in a cellar.

Now I was braver. I could creep closer to the library and have a quick look inside. Without puking. Though once I saw Edna, I just about lost my dessert.

Edna was tied to Birdie's chair by the fireplace. A piece of duct tape covered her mouth. Her hair was wrecked, and tears stained the front of her shirt.

Did someone do this to her?

Or was this another trap?

I turned to Nathalie. She motioned again for me to hurry. But my heart wouldn't let me. I shook my head *no*. Amelia had stopped once during an air race to help a friend who'd crashed, and I was going to help Edna. I couldn't leave her like this.

Edna's eyes met mine. They grew wide with surprise. I tiptoed into the room and across the rug, past the spot where Birdie had fallen a few hours before. Collin's taxidermy textbook sat on the coffee table, splayed open, next to an empty plate and fork. In spite of everything my stomach growled.

I pointed to the tape across her mouth, and Edna nodded. "Sorry," I said as I gripped the edge and ripped it off.

"Ugh. Where are the others?" she asked.

"In the breezeway. Well, three of them are." I untied her wrists. My heart hurt, thinking about Thea and Wren. I hoped they were safe. I hoped they'd found the police.

Edna looked alarmed. "Three? What about the other two? Where's Collin?"

My stomach dropped. "Locked in the cellar," I whispered.

"What?" Edna looked horrified.

"I'll explain later. First, let's get out of here."

"Millie, you have to listen to me." Edna swallowed. "It's Perry. *He* locked you in the basement. *He* tied me up. Not Collin. Perry's the dangerous one. You need to get out. *Now.*"

"No one's going anywhere." Perry stumbled through the doorway, carrying a small backpack. "But me, that is. As soon as Millie tells me where the goggles are. The *real* ones." His voice was low.

"I'm sorry?" I croaked.

"You heard me." Perry drilled his eyes into me. I shuddered.

Edna, bless her, slipped in front of me. "She doesn't owe you anything, Perry. If you want something, you can talk to me."

Perry dropped his bag. It wasn't zipped, and cooking utensils spilled onto the floor. I had a hunch these items— a giant whisk, wooden spatulas, and what appeared to be a handheld blender—belonged to Birdie instead of him. Still, I gulped at the sight of the butcher's knife. "Whoops." He smirked.

In a flash, Edna kicked the blade underneath Grandma Otis's velvet sofa. I went from hating Edna's guts eight hours ago to becoming her number-one fan. I was pretty sure she could kill Perry with her pinky if she decided to.

"Aww, shucks. That was my favorite knife." His sarcasm quickly switched to irritation. "I guess I'll have to use my other one." He whipped out a pocketknife.

I gulped.

"I didn't come all the way back to Kansas for nothing, Millie. Tell me where the goggles are."

Someone sneezed. Once; twice; three times. Electra dashed across the floor.

I closed my eyes. *Robin.* What was she doing here? I thought she'd run next door.

Perry turned toward the sound, and cement filled my throat.

"Come out, come out, wherever you are, you little brats," he thundered, slashing his knife through the air. "Don't you know friends stick together?"

Friends.

I didn't have friends until I came here. I had a family, my dad. But no friends.

Robin appeared in the adjacent doorway first, tearful and trembling. Then Cassie, her face set with resolve. Nathalie emerged last. She held Rosie Stancer up to her chest.

I shook my head, unable to speak. Unable to scream.

I'd been so busy worrying about myself I hadn't even noticed they'd waited for me.

"Perry, don't do this," Edna said. "Put the knife down, and everyone goes home."

Home.

Home was with Dad. My dad always knew what to do in a crisis. I thought back to the last time I'd seen him, in his beanie, lugging Danni the Body and reluctant to leave me overnight. I thought about the awkward, shy smile he'd shown Kate. And I realized something. My dad needed me like I needed him.

My friends needed me.

Shoot, even Amelia Earhart, wherever she was, needed me. I couldn't let this jerk run off with anything of hers.

I had to do something. *Think, Millie, think.*

My brain kicked into high gear.

I couldn't stop Perry, but I could slow him down.

"Let's make a deal. I'll tell you where the goggles are, if you answer a few questions for me. But first you have to lose the knife."

Perry grunted. "What kind of questions?"

"Easy ones," I answered.

Perry's eyes narrowed. "You got yourself a deal." He tossed the knife onto the floor.

Holy moly. I blinked.

Edna rushed to retrieve the knife, and the butterflies in my stomach swarmed.

"Go on, I don't have all night," Perry growled.

"Right." I swallowed and reached into my hoodie's pocket for my beloved cube. Suddenly, I felt as small as Rosie Stancer. I was just a puny kid with a puzzle toy, standing up to an adult. I wasn't brave like Amelia Earhart. But I had her name, and that was a solid start.

Then, from the corner of my eye, I saw Robin calmly lift her phone to record.

You can be quiet and brave.

CHAPTER THIRTY-TWO

Perry shook his head at me and scoffed. "What's this? Playtime?"

I shrugged. "You promised me a solve, remember?" I shoved my hands back inside my pockets to hide their trembling.

Perry picked up my cube and snorted. At the very least I was buying the police precious seconds to arrive.

"So," I began, "exactly when did you leave the warning note? That was smart to use the mannequin."

Perry twisted the yellow face first. "What makes you think that was me?"

I pretended to scratch my neck. "Oh, you know, the handwriting matched the dinner menu. And you had the perfect chance to swipe Collin's scalpel after he accidentally left it by the fruit after slicing an orange."

Perry turned my cube over and scrutinized the squares.

I noticed a burn mark on the back of his hand.

"Second question. What's with your tattoo?" I asked.

"What about it?" Perry asked, twisting my cube faster.

"What's the story? Why that particular plane?"

"That's none of your business," he barked.

"You've made it my business by holding us hostage." My voice shook. Who was I?

"You girls had bad timing, that's all." Perry shook his head in irritation. I couldn't tell if it was due to my cube or my question. "Amelia ran low on fuel during her transcontinental flight and made an emergency landing in a spot on the map called McNeal, Arizona, where some of my family's from. This was the plane. It's the Avro Avian she bought while touring Britain after the *Friendship* crossing."

"That's incredible," I said. "Only it's not her plane."

"Yes it is," he barked. "You don't know anything."

"Amelia's Avro Avian had the aircraft marking G-EBUG. Your tattoo says G-EB*OV*. You mistakenly got a tattoo of an Australian pilot's plane. There are some old models in the cellar, if you'd like to double-check." I paused to let the news sink in. I won't lie; it felt pretty great to explain he'd tatted the wrong plane. "Your phony interest in Amelia might have fooled Birdie and the Ninety-Nines, but it won't fool me. Or my friends."

Perry huffed and turned my cube with so much force I thought he'd break it. "So, the tattoo artist messed up. Big deal. Are we done yet?" he snapped.

Thea's lucky bracelet clung to my wrist. We needed the police, ASAP. *Where are you, Thea?*

Edna shot me a warning look.

"Almost," I said, faking a smile. "That burn looks like it hurts."

Perry glanced down at the back of his hand. "Breaker box," he muttered. "Now, where are those goggles?"

Breaker box. My heart skipped. Perry was a chef. A burn from the stove was to be expected, but one from the circuit breaker was not.

"Okay. Last question," I said, buzzing with more energy than Times Square. "Did you *plan* on drugging Birdie from the very start, or was it simply an impromptu decision after the goggles disappeared?"

Perry slammed my cube down. I jumped.

"Game over. Give me the goggles. Now."

"I, uh, just need a minute." My brain scrambled. I couldn't think. I was terrified.

Edna filled the silence. "We're not giving you the goggles, Perry. But if you talk, and are agreeable, things will go better for you."

"I didn't hurt her, okay?" Perry shouted. "It's just an herb. Anyone can buy it over the counter. I just need the goggles, then I'll take off."

"Which was all you wanted in the first place, so you could auction them off and use the money to attend your precious culinary school!" I said. "Only someone beat you to it. Someone stole the goggles first. But you couldn't stand being outsmarted. So, you created a diversion. You slipped some of Collin's valerian into Birdie's tea. If she was asleep and everyone else was scared off, you'd have time to find them and steal them back. But we meddled. So, you left us a handwritten warning. Your first mistake."

"What about the crushed peppermint?" asked Cassie.

I shook my head. "Planted. He took it from the ginger-bread house to make it look like Edna was working with Collin."

Edna's mouth fell open.

Perry snickered. "Pretty smart, if you ask me."

"Very," I said. "And you were as cool as an ice cube until you heard we'd found the goggles. Then you panicked, hurried into the basement, and messed with the main breaker switch, leaving us in the dark."

"You can't prove it," he spouted.

"You said so yourself, about your burn mark. And why else would you tie up Edna? With us locked in the basement and Birdie snoozing, all you'd have left was to drug Collin or knock him out. Then you could snag the goggles and run." I didn't dare share that we'd knocked Collin out for him.

"No." His nostrils flared. "You're wrong. You're just a kid. You're all wrong!" He flailed his arms in a rage, knocking over Amelia's walnut table. The contents crashed to the floor.

"You don't know what it's like to work around the clock and barely scrape by. To wash dishes until your hands blister and bleed, and you still can't keep the lights on. I didn't come from money, but no one's worked harder than I did to get into culinary school. No. One. I got in. On my own. I deserve to go."

"Not like this," Edna said, and unwrapped a mint. "There are other ways. More noble ones." She calmly placed the mint on her tongue.

Perry's cheeks flushed red. His eyes flashed wild. He lunged at Edna, grabbing her arm and twisting it behind her.

She yelped in surprise.

"Hey! That's not necessary," I said.

Edna scrabbled and fought, but Perry's grip was strong.

"Perry, stop!" I shouted.

Nathalie and Cassie screamed, and Robin started to cry.

"Shut up! All of you!" Perry barked, backing up with Edna. "I'm not a criminal! If anyone's a criminal, it's Birdie. She's the one who stole the goggles."

The goggles.

I knew then there was only one way to end this nightmare. I reached into my hoodie pocket and grabbed the goggles. The real ones. The ones Amelia Earhart had called historic. The ones she liked because they fit her "unconventional" nose. I hoped she would forgive me.

"You win," I said.

Perry's lip curled. He sneered. "That's a good girl. Now hand them over."

"No! Rosie!" Nathalie yelled as Rosie Stancer leapt from her pocket onto the wood floor.

We all glanced down, and Edna took advantage of that split second to stomp on Perry's foot.

Still, something about her didn't look right. For the first time in this whole horrid night, Edna looked scared. No, terrified. Her eyes bulged out of their sockets. Her lips looked purple. If I knew anything from my classes with Dad, Edna was in respiratory distress.

"Let her go! She's choking! She's *choking!*"

Sweat appeared on Perry's forehead. "Give me the goggles!"

I looked at Edna. I looked at my friends. *Oh, heck no.* I wasn't going down without a fight.

"Fine. You want the goggles?" I screamed. "Come and get them yourself." And I flung the precious tinted lenses with aluminum frames into the air.

Perry dove, and Edna stumbled forward, her hands clutching her throat. I wrapped my arms around her waist. Making a fist, I thrust my hands one, two, three, four times fast into her abdomen, practically lifting her off the ground.

The peppermint shot out of her mouth.

Pure adrenaline. That's all there was to that.

"Thank you," Edna said, gulping air.

Right as a siren wailed.

CHAPTER THIRTY-THREE

"Don't you even think about leaving with those goggles," a voice said.

I turned my head and could hardly believe my eyes.

Birdie stood in front of the mahogany staircase, still lit with holiday garlands. Her left hand was raised in the air. Her right hand wielded a long sword. She must have grabbed it from the wall on her way down. My jaw dropped as she shuffled forward. Birdie was a boss.

"Birdie?" Perry took a slow step back. "We can talk through this."

Birdie trained the foil on Perry's chest. I almost laughed at the sight of Perry scuttling backward like a crab as Birdie prodded him. The tip of her blade tickled his shirt. Birdie meant business.

"Put the goggles down before I slice off your schnoz."

Perry gulped and laid the goggles on the rug.

Birdie grunted. "Good. Now, get out!"

Perry jumped up and ran straight out the front door, down the porch steps, and into the Atchison Police force.

"Freeze!" they yelled. "You are under arrest."

The next few moments were a blur. Edna hurried to meet the officers outside while I rushed to see the other girls.

Robin, still clutching her phone, had passed out cold from fright.

An idea came to me. "Cassie, do you still have Amelia's smelling salts?"

She smiled. "I thought you'd never ask."

"You were amazing, Millie," Nathalie said, wrapping me in a hug.

"Thanks. Did you find Rosie?"

She pointed to the floor. Rosie was busy burrowing beneath the broken table and a spilled vase of flowers.

"Rosie's a little traumatized, but she's doing what she does best—scouting for food and treasure. See? She's already found something."

Rosie held up a shiny piece of metal.

"Birdie's gold earring! Edna must have dropped it in the skirmish. Well done, Rosie." I took the jewelry from her itty pink paws and, despite my fear of rats, managed to give her a lightning-quick pat.

Then Robin's phone buzzed, and she sat up. "Hey, I missed a call from—"

"Wren! Thea!"

"Ashford!" The girls rushed into the house, and I nearly cried. Oh my goggles, was it good to see them. I gave them both the biggest bear hug.

"You have to tell us everything," said Thea.

"I will," I promised, "but first Wren needs to see her sister. She captured the whole confession on her phone."

I stepped aside, and Wren's face broke into a grin. "Way to go, Robin," she said, giving her a hug.

Robin laughed. "Thanks. And thank goodness for Amelia's smelling salts."

"Speaking of which, I need to turn those and this earring over to the police."

"That shouldn't be hard. The place is crawling with cops." Wren grabbed my arm right as an officer slid past us, talking into his mic. I shook my head, unable to take it all in. Then Wren directed my attention out the door and across the yard.

Red and blue lights pierced the night. A handcuffed Perry ducked into the back of a police cruiser. He looked at us briefly through the window, then turned away.

My stomach clenched. Meanwhile, in the glow of an old gas lamp, Birdie talked to the chief of police. She looked so frail and small next to the cops. The opposite of the spitfire who'd flown stunts and, moments ago, wielded a sword.

A mustached man in a long black coat walked over. His jacket had silver snaps down the front, and a shiny badge on his chest caught the flashing emergency lights.

"I'm Detective Borkowski. I'm sorry you kids have been through so much, but once your guardians arrive, I'll need to ask you a few questions." He smiled apologetically. His left cheek had a small scar, like he'd nicked it once while shaving.

"Sure. But you should know Robin captured the whole confession on her phone. And we accidentally left Collin in the cellar." My ears burned hot. "We thought he was a bad guy."

Detective Borkowski threw his head back and laughed. "You mean Lieutenant Stewart? Officer Jones tipped us off. You kids sure gave him a run for his money."

Huh. Edna must be Officer Jones. "So, he's all right?" I asked.

Detective Borkowski chuckled. "He's got a few bruised ribs, but he'll recover. You can talk to him if you want." He pointed behind me. I swiveled around to see Collin sitting on a stretcher in the back of an ambulance. He was talking with Edna, who'd brought him a cup of water. He looked up, saw me, and waved.

I gave him a sheepish smile and waved back.

"Thanks. Oh, and, Detective?" I dug into my pocket. "We

found this earring near the empty display case. It belongs to Birdie."

Detective Borkowski studied the tiny bird and nodded. "Nice sleuthing. Now, if you kids will excuse me for a moment."

"Sure." I shrugged. "But first, would it be all right if I talked to Birdie?"

"I don't see why not." The detective spoke into his radio and stepped outside. A minute later Birdie appeared on the porch, gripping a thermos of hot tea.

"Don't worry. A neighbor down the way brewed it," she said, laughing softly. A heavy fleece engulfed her shoulders, and tears welled up in her eyes. "I've aged ten years in one night." She paused and squeezed my hand. "Millie, can you ever forgive me?"

I nodded, not really sure what to say or if I was really ready to forgive just yet. But I liked Birdie, still. I knew that much.

The other girls gathered around us, and Birdie took a deep breath.

"I owe all of you girls and your parents an apology. And the Ninety-Nines. I've let you, your families, and my sisters—my fellow fliers—down. I never meant to cause such chaos and harm." Her voice broke, and she looked down. "I simply meant to keep Amelia's goggles with the family, so to speak. They were the heart of the house. The main attraction. What the guests were most excited about. I was afraid visitors would stop coming if the goggles moved elsewhere. . . . So, I panicked and hid them. I foolishly thought a little excitement over their 'disappearance' couldn't hurt and would bring us some needed press. Boy, was I wrong." She sipped her tea.

"What did you plan to do with the goggles? Hide them forever?" asked Wren.

"Oh goodness, no. I'm not a thief."

"But you misled people," said Robin.

"That I did. And I'm sorry. I was going to return the goggles—anonymously, of course. I'd call the papers with my discovery, make a big fuss, then use the media blitz to announce a petition to keep the goggles here."

"But, Birdie, even more people can enjoy them in Washington."

"You're absolutely right, Millie. I see that now."

"I understand why you did it," Thea said. "Not that you should have, but I understand your wanting to keep them here."

"Thanks, Thea." Birdie's smile was sad. "Still, it was misguided, and I'm sorry."

I cleared my throat. "I do have one question, Birdie, if you don't mind my asking."

"Go on."

"Why the Christmas tree? Why not your apartment or the freezer or a million other hiding places?"

Birdie smiled, for real this time. "Because I adore Christmas! And my apartment would have been too obvious."

"Okay. My turn," said Cassie. "Birdie, I didn't see you upstairs when I retrieved Robin's medicine at dinner. Shouldn't I have at least passed you in the hallway or on the stairs?"

Birdie laughed. "I took the secret passage! I'd hoped you girls would have found it by now."

"Oh, we have." Thea shuddered, and everyone laughed.

"Excuse me, Ms. Anderson. We need to ask you a few more questions." A policewoman came and led Birdie away right as a van pulled up. Nathalie and I watched as the side door slid open and a crowd spilled out, running to the house.

"Mills!"

My heart leapt into my throat. I'd know that voice, that beanie, anywhere. It was my favorite voice in the whole wide world. "Dad!"

I flew down the front steps and into his arms.

"Millie! I'm so glad you're okay."

"Me too, Dad. Me too."

Next to me, Mrs. Lam showered Cassie with kisses, and a couple, who had to be the Winterses, rushed to hug their daughters.

"We did it, Ashford," Wren said.

"We did. I knew I could count on you. All of you." I looked up at my friends.

"Millie, there's someone special I want you to meet." Dad

motioned to an older woman holding a steaming cup of coffee and wearing a rich red scarf. "This is Nina Hegg, president of the Ninety-Nines. She sent you your invitation. She was supposed to be here earlier, but her travel was delayed."

"Nice to meet you, Ms. Hegg," I said, sticking out my hand.

"Likewise, Millie. But please call me Nina." Her eyes twinkled, and her grip was strong. "Or Java, like your mom does." She winked.

A grin spread across my face. "No way. *You're* Java?"

"The one and only." She held up her coffee and grinned.

"You taught my mom to fly."

"I did!" Java laughed. "She had the worst case of nerves I'd ever seen in a cadet!"

I wrinkled my nose. "But my mom wasn't afraid of anything."

Snowflakes landed on Java's eyelashes, and she smiled like she was sharing a secret. "Child, your mom missed her first solo because she was in the bathroom, sick. She almost earned the name 'Pukes,' but because she flew with a lucky penny in her boot, 'Lucky' stuck."

"'Lucky' Penny Ashford. I never knew that." A lump formed in my throat. I couldn't bring up Hong Kong. Not yet. "Do you see her much?"

"It's been years." Java touched the tip of my nose. "But she would be so proud of you, kid."

"I know I am." Dad put his arm around me right as a fashionable lady in tall boots, a puffy coat, and glossy red lips bustled over. She was holding a microphone.

"Hello, I'm Caryn Chinn with Channel Five News. May I ask you girls a few questions?"

Wren's face lit up like a shooting star. "Sure. My subscribers will love this. Do you mind if I snap a quick picture?"

CHAPTER THIRTY-FOUR

The sun rose at precisely 7:03 in the morning, and even though it'd been the longest night ever, Dad and I showed up to breakfast five minutes ahead of schedule. The Atchison Inn, with its cheery indoor plants, piles of books, and hot cider, was much more welcoming at daybreak than in the dead of night. This was good, considering the girls and I were meeting various administrators and reporters over doughnuts soon. It was a big news day for the small town of Atchison, and the majority of the residents were sleeping in or snuggled by the fire, blissfully unaware.

I had just poured myself a glass of freshly squeezed orange juice when Java wrapped me in a hug. I smiled. She really did smell like coffee at all hours.

"Are you ready for the presser?" she asked.

"Presser?" I said, suddenly feeling nervous. "What's that?"

She laughed. "Press conference! Remember, relax and be yourself. You'll do great."

"Okay. Thanks." I smiled with relief. Once, when I was nine, my picture made the local newspaper for winning a cubing competition. But this press conference was nothing compared to that. There were cameras and reporters from all over the region, if not the country. The room was already feeling too small.

Java put her hand on my arm. "Before I forget, don't forget to look for your brick at the house. They should have shoveled the front walk in anticipation of the crowd."

"What brick? And what crowd?" I wrinkled my nose.

"Don't tell me you don't know!" Java shook her head. "Make your dad promise to take you back when the weather's better. And by 'crowd,' I mean journalists and gawkers. This is the most happening thing that's happened to Atchison since Amelia's parade in 1935!" She winked.

"Okay. Got it." I wiped juice from my mouth and smiled.

Java held up her coffee in salute. "See you in a few, kid. You know? You're all right."

I couldn't help but laugh. Because wherever the goggles wound up, I knew Java and the Ninety-Nines would make sure they were all right too.

After stuffing myself with too many doughnuts, it was time to answer more questions than a standardized test.

I found my seat next to Nathalie and Wren at a long table in front of a stone fireplace. All six of us had microphones, like we were ambassadors to the UN. Rows of reporters, journalists, and cameramen faced us. This wasn't so bad. At least I was with friends.

Dad waved to me from the back and gave me a thumbs-up. Java took a moment to thank everyone for being there, then left the microphone to Detective Borkowski, whom we'd met last night. If it wasn't for his mustache, I wouldn't have recognized him. He'd combed his hair back and traded his police coat for a button-down, blazer, and bags under both eyes. Someone handed him a coffee. He nodded thanks, then stepped to the mic.

"Good morning. I'm Detective John Borkowski with the Atchison Police Department's Criminal Investigative Division. Here with me are Officer Edna Jones and Chief of Police Jason Gonzales. Before I start, good morning to the chief, staff, media, Mayor Justus, and our six brave guests: Millie, Nathalie, Wren, Robin, Thea, and Cassie. First, a little background as to why we're here . . ."

My mind wandered as the detective summarized the events of last night. I wished I'd brought my cube. But I didn't, so I scanned the room instead. There was Edna, standing off to the side, in her pressed navy police uniform. She'd pulled her hair back and put on a tie. Ten bucks says she had a peppermint. She saw me looking and winked.

I'd heard Collin wasn't feeling well enough to make it. I felt a little bad for him, but not too much. He'd started out as a creep. Maybe he'd be kinder to people from now on, including his aunt. Still, it has to be hard seeing people you love make such public mistakes.

Oh, Birdie.

It was hard to imagine her masterminding a grand plan to steal Amelia's goggles. Part of me felt sorry for her, possibly trading her historic home for a jail cell. She meant well. But good intentions don't make wrongs right. Then again, who knows what would have happened to the goggles—and us—had she not appeared at the end?

"And now we'll take a few questions," announced Detective B. "Channel Five, we'll start with you."

Caryn, the stylish reporter we'd posed with, stood up. "Good morning, Detective. My first question is for the girls." Caryn turned to us and smiled. "Is it true that some of you escaped and ran to get help? If so, how? And were you scared?"

We all looked at one another. No one wanted to go first.

Wren leaned into her microphone and grinned. "Thea can take this one."

"Gee, thanks." Thea laughed.

The journalists chuckled, and I smiled. They understood we were nervous.

"To answer your question, yes," Thea said. "It's true. Wren and I escaped through a basement window. First, we ran to a neighbor's house, but no one was home. We thought about breaking a window. Well, Wren did." Thea laughed.

"We were running on adrenaline!" said Wren.

Thea nodded. "We could keep trying houses and pray that someone heard us or run the five blocks to the police station. In the end, we didn't have time to be scared. We had to get help."

"We also found an old suitcase of Amelia's in the cellar and layered on her flight suits to stay warm," said Wren.

Caryn's eyebrows shot up. "Amazing. Where are the flight suits now?"

Thea shrugged. The room exploded in laughter.

Detective B spoke into his microphone, "To be clear, the Ninety-Nines have them and will incorporate them into a display at a later date."

Caryn sat down, and another journalist, with flyaway hair and Nebraska News credentials, put her hand into the air.

"Yes," called the detective.

She stood. "Thank you, Detective. Is it true a suspect was taken into custody last night?"

Detective B nodded. "Yes, we have two individuals— a white female and a white male—in custody. Both are cooperating with the investigation. But the important part is the goggles have been recovered safely, thanks to these kids."

More hands shot into the air. More phones, more cameras aimed toward our faces.

"Lou." Detective Borkowski pointed to a potbellied reporter in an *Atchison Daily Globe* shirt and suspenders.

Lou cleared his throat. "Detective, can you confirm that the goggles are still headed to the Smithsonian?"

"Yes. Representatives from the National Air and Space Museum are en route. Next?" The detective took a sip of coffee.

Caryn with Channel Five popped up. "Detective, my sources say one individual was treated and released at the county hospital overnight. Can you confirm?"

Detective B nodded. "One officer was treated for minor scrapes and bruises. A concussion was ruled out. A second officer was saved from choking before we arrived."

"Thank you, sir," Caryn replied. "One final question, for the girls. What did you do, once you realized the goggles were missing?"

Nathalie nudged me.

"Panic?" I laughed. "I'd seen the goggles in the case earlier that evening, so I knew something was wrong. But we were also doing this scavenger hunt, so we thought maybe they'd been moved as part of the game. So, we called everyone upstairs and decided to split up to search the house."

Lou called out, "Where did you finally find the goggles?"

I leaned into the mic. "The Christmas tree."

More laughs.

Detective B motioned for quiet. "Thank you, Millie. Before we conclude this conference, the mayor would like to present each of the girls with a key to the city as a token of our appreciation."

What?

I looked at my friends in disbelief as Mayor Justus rose and gave each of us a golden key. Each key had Atchison's city logo and Amelia's profile imprinted on top.

Bulbs flashed like fireworks, and the journalists rose to their feet in applause. What. A. Morning. I'd never felt so happy, proud, and exhausted.

After the presser wrapped and I'd shaken my one hundredth hand, I had one last request. "Dad, would you take a picture of me with my friends?"

"Sure. Everyone scrunch together and look this way. Okay. Say 'keys'!"

"Keys!"

Click.

We all swapped phone numbers, and before any of us were truly ready, it was time to say goodbye.

Outside, an engine revved.

"Thea!" someone called.

Thea rolled her eyes. "That's my aunt. I've got to go, guys."

"Thea! What about your lucky bracelet?" I yelled over the roar of the bike.

She strapped on her helmet and grinned. "You keep it."

A sleek SUV pulled up beside us. The driver got out and waited patiently by the back door.

"Well, that's my ride," said Cassie, even though we all knew it was. "I guess my parents finished schmoozing with the lawyers." She laughed a little apologetically, then rushed to give us each a hug. "You are all invited to visit me in Houston. I mean it."

"Thanks," I said.

"Hey, Millie. Look for our livestream!" Wren shouted as she as Robin climbed into their parents' van.

"Well, my dad's waiting too. See you later, Millie," Nathalie said. She cradled her pet rat. "Have a safe trip home."

"You too, Nathalie. And hey, I hope you get to visit your mom in Antarctica."

She pulled her pet rat from her pocket and smiled. "And I hope you get to visit yours—if you want to, I mean."

"Thanks. Maybe someday." I reached out and patted Rosie Stancer on the head. "It was so nice meeting you, Rosie. You're the first, and only, rat I've liked."

Not long after, I was sitting on the porch of the Atchison Inn, reading travel brochures and waiting for Dad to arrive with our car. Tow Truck Tom had left a voice mail saying he'd pulled it free from the ditch. Then a reporter had offered to drive Dad back over the bridge to pick it up. Now, here I sat, sipping hot cider in the afternoon sun, deep into a story about Atchison being the most-haunted town in Kansas—which I'm so glad I didn't know yesterday, and I'm

100 percent sending this pamphlet to Thea—when a horn honked. I jumped. I mean, I was just reading about ghosts. And there was Kate from New Horizons Poultry, waving from her empty turkey truck.

"Millie! I saw the news!" she yelled, climbing down from the cab. "I'm so glad you're okay. I brought you some Twizzlers. Where's your dad? I want to hear everything."

Kate couldn't believe my story and sat patiently while I told her every last detail. I told her about sharing the Twizzlers, making the decoy mannequins, and setting the tomato juice trap in the basement. I even mentioned the valerian and Cassie's family's greenhouse and how an orange zinnia was the first flower to bloom in space. I think she liked that. Then, before I knew it, Dad's car puttered into the parking lot.

I lugged my duffel bag to the car and watched Kate and dad laugh together on the porch. Of course, Danni was there too. But for once Dad wasn't paying him any attention.

"All ready to go, Mills?" Dad called, shielding his eyes from the sun.

I slipped my hand into my coat pocket. "Yeah, Dad. There's one thing I have to do first."

"Okay, but make it quick. Kate knows this great pizza place, and more snow's blowing in tonight."

I nodded and sprinted across the lot to the front of the inn. Stomping up the steps, I stopped at the entrance, in front of a big iron mailbox. I reached into my pocket and pulled out the postcard and stamp I'd bought at Amelia's birthplace. The postcard had a nice photograph of the home on the front. The grass was green. Leaves clung to the trees. I could almost hear birds chirping. Changing seasons were a part of life. I stuck the stamp on the back and skimmed what I had written:

Dear Mom:

Hi. I found your new address in a Ninety-Nines directory at Amelia Earhart's birthplace. I met your old friend Java. She's great. I also saved someone from choking, stopped a robbery, and got my picture in the newspaper—all with help from my new friends and a rat named Rosie. Maybe someday I can come to Hong Kong and tell you everything in person. But for now, I'm sticking to adventures in books. Dad's waiting on me, so bye.

Your daughter,
Millie

I dropped the card into the mail slot and ran back to meet Kate and Dad. If Mom wanted to reach out to me, she could.

I pulled out my cube and caught a glimpse of Mom's pilot wings pinned to my jacket. Then I saw my shiny new pin fastened next to hers, and my heart exploded like a million stars. I looked up at the clear blue sky and squinted, right as a plane roared overhead. I might have imagined it, but I swore it tipped its wings in greeting.

I waved my arms and laughed as the winter sun warmed my face and the Kansas wind whipped through my hair.

"Thanks, Amelia. Adventure really is worthwhile."

Six months later.

Wren: Hello, explorers! It's Wren.

Robin: And I'm Robin! Welcome to another episode of the Mars Millen. Today we're in Houston, Texas, visiting some superspecial guests. You may have heard about them already.

Wren: If you're a longtime explorer, you've definitely heard us talk about them.

Robin: Definitely. [Laughs.] Remember when Wren and I spent the night at Amelia Earhart's birthplace?

Wren: It was bananas.

Robin: Bananas. But we made some great friends.

Wren: We did! And the four other girls—Cassie, Millie, Nathalie, and Thea—are here with us today! [Camera pans to group.]

All: Hi! [Laughter.]

Robin: So, we're staying in Houston with Cassie Lam and learning all about her family's Space Farming Initiative with NASA. Cool, huh?

Cassie: Hi, everyone. I'm Cassie. Welcome to Houston. [Waves.]

Wren: We'll have a future episode dedicated to Cassie's garden. So, stay tuned! But today we wanted to talk about what happened after our time in Kansas. As some of you know, the trial just ended.

Thea: Hi. Thea here. Some of you may be asking, "What trial?" So, here's a quick recap: The six of us were invited to spend the night last winter at the Amelia Earhart Birthplace Museum in Atchison, Kansas. We had a scavenger hunt indoors, while a blizzard raged outside—

Wren: A total blizzard! We lost power, and—

Thea: Amelia's flight goggles disappeared.

Cassie: True.

Millie: Hi, I'm Millie. [Holding her Rubik's Cube.] Other stuff happened too. Crazy stuff. Like, we found a secret passageway.

Wren: Because WHO KNEW Amelia's grandparents helped freedom seekers along the Underground Railroad? Not me.

Robin: [Points to herself.] Not me. But they did.

Nathalie: Hi. I'm Nathalie, and this is Rosie. Then the

scariest thing happened. We got trapped in the basement, and Wren and Thea had to sneak out a window to get help.

Wren: We ran five blocks in the cold! At least it was downhill. Mostly.

Thea: I'm just glad we survived and saw zero ghosts. Though the police chief thought he was seeing things when we showed up in Amelia's flight suits.

[Laughter.]

Wren: Hey, they kept us warm.

Millie: I bet.

Robin: [Nodding.] *But.* We found the goggles! Well, Millie did.

Millie: With everyone's help.

Wren: She totally did! Mystery solved. But lots has happened since. Birdie, the museum's caretaker, confessed to plotting to keep the goggles at the house. She's since stepped down and moved in with her daughter. The Ninety-Nines, the International Organization of Women Pilots, decided against pressing charges and are appointing someone new to take her place. We're secretly hoping they choose one of us. [Laughter.]

Nathalie: And what about Chef Perry?

Thea: Perry was charged and found guilty on multiple counts—threatening a minor, assaulting a police officer, intent to inflict bodily harm, and unlawful imprisonment of others. He's sentenced to two years in jail. Weirdly, that's the duration of some culinary schools.

Cassie: Sheesh. At least it's over, and the museum can move on. What will happen to Electra, Birdie's cat?

Millie: Birdie's family is allergic, so Electra's moved in with me.

Wren: Aww. That makes for a happy ending. Check out the Mars Millennium webpage for pictures of the house and to view never-before-seen footage from that night. There's also a link to our interview in the local newspaper, the *Atchison Daily Globe*, and a close-up photograph of our commemorative Amelia Six brick embedded in the walkway outside the home.

Robin: Ah-mazing. But you know what, friends? There is *some* unfinished business.

Cassie: There is?

Robin: Yup. The museum's scavenger hunt. Millie saved her checklist! See? [Camera zooms in.]

Wren: I can't believe you kept that! We were so going to win.

Millie: We were close all right, but there are two items we never filled in. I thought it'd be fun to read them here.

Wren: Okay. I'm ready.

Millie: Here we go. First riddle: Find and name Amelia's favorite childhood toy. You might say it's as stubborn as a mule.

Robin: Oh, that's a good one! Does anyone know?

Nathalie: [Waves.] I do! Amelia's favorite toy was a wooden donkey she called Donk.

Millie: Great job, Nathalie! Now for the second one. Are you ready?

All: Yes!

Millie: Okay. This one is harder. An early adopter, Amelia used *this* method of transportation to zip around airports at a whopping fifteen miles per hour.

Cassie: Hmm. A bicycle?

Millie: No. But good guess. It has the same number of wheels.

Thea: In that case, it has to be an electric scooter.

Millie: Yes! That's it.

Robin: Hooray! For even *more* information on Amelia Earhart, because she is incredible, visit your local library or bookshop. Don't forget to take your reading list.*

Nathalie: Be sure to join us next time as we head to the South Pole to talk climate change and penguins with my mom, an Antarctic scientist.

Wren: Way cool. Literally.

Robin: Ha! Yes. Brrr. Keep exploring, friends, and remember . . .

All: Adventure awaits!

*A Mars Millennium reading list for all things Amelia Earhart:

Amelia Lost: The Life and Disappearance of Amelia Earhart by Candace Fleming

Night Flight: Amelia Earhart Crosses the Atlantic by Robert Burleigh and Wendell Minor

Amelia and Eleanor Go for a Ride by Pam Muñoz Ryan and Brian Selznick

Who Was Amelia Earhart? by Kate Boehm Jerome and David Cain

Amelia Earhart: Young Aviator by Beatrice Gormley and Meryl Henderson

Amelia Earhart: A Photographic Story of a Life by Tanya Lee Stone

The Last Grand Adventure by Rebecca Behrens (historical fiction)

And for the truly ambitious reader:

20 Hrs., 40 Min.: Our Flight in the Friendship by Amelia Earhart

For information on Rubik's Cube solutions and speedcubing, visit youcandothecube.com, worldcubeassociation.org, and rubiks.com.

Author's Note

The summer after third grade, my family visited the Smithsonian National Air and Space Museum in Washington, DC, I saw the Wright brothers' airplane up close. I marveled at Apollo's Lunar Module LM-2. I tried my first bite of astronaut ice cream (and was sorely disappointed). Amelia's red Lockheed Vega 5B, which she flew on her historic solo transatlantic flight, was there at the time, though I don't recall seeing it. But I do know something shifted in me during that trip. I developed a new respect and deep admiration for aviation, space, and the brave explorers who dared.

When it came time to think about writing this book, I knew I wanted to attempt a mystery. Mysteries were my favorite books to read as a child, and writing one proved harder than I ever expected! But I was fixated on the idea of setting a mystery in a place that existed in real life, not just inside my imagination. I wanted a place that readers could visit and experience beyond the page. I had a few ideas, but after taking a holiday road trip, the Amelia Earhart Birthplace Museum rose to the top. The concept of an all-girl cast excited me. Amelia and the Ninety-Nines worked tirelessly to encourage women to go into aviation and engineering-related fields, as well as to simply take a leap of faith by purchasing commercial airline tickets! The airline industry was in its infancy, and many people were afraid to fly. Amelia and her peers broke barriers and set countless records striving to make air travel safe and accessible for all. Airline passengers today are forever in their debt.

While I tried to present Amelia herself as accurately as possible, I'd be remiss if I did not note a few changes I made for the sake of the story:

In 2009, Amelia's goggles from her 1932 solo transatlantic flight went up for auction. This sale also included Amelia's thank-you letter to Ray Fernstrom, as well as letters from Purdue University and the Smithsonian. Both institutions had hoped to add the goggles to their permanent collection. Though obviously no crime was committed, these ideas combined in my mind to spark Millie's story. As for the auction? An anonymous bidder won. A mere $141,600 must be a small price to pay for a piece of aviation history.

Yes, Judge and Amelia Otis's home is believed to have been a stop on the Kansas Underground Railroad. While I invented the secret passageway, later research revealed the judge probably installed a trapdoor in the parlor floor (covered by a rug), which led into the cellar. I took the liberty of switching the front (women's) parlor and the library to take advantage of the marble fireplace. I also added an upstairs bath. And while I did not directly address the mysterious disappearance of Amelia and her Lockheed 10-E (many others have), it seems important to mention here what we do know.

Facts: Amelia and her navigator, Fred Noonan, left Lae, New Guinea, for Howland Island on the morning of July 2, 1937, and were never seen again. Howland was to be one of the last refueling stops on their around-the-world flight. A treeless, banana-shaped island, Howland is uninhabited and only 1.5 miles (2.4 km) long. A dot in the Pacific Ocean, it is situated halfway between Hawaii and Australia and is a territory of the United States.

The United States Coast Guard sent a patrol boat, the *Itasca*, to the island to help guide Amelia, and left eighteen drums of fuel near the crude landing strip.

According to the ship's logs, Amelia radioed that she couldn't see the island, couldn't hear the ship, and was running low on fuel:

Earhart on now; says she is running out of gas, only 1/2 hour left, can't hear us at all. We hear her and are sending on 3105 and 500 at the same time, constantly.

Then, at 8:43 a.m. local time, the *Itasca* received its last radio transmission from Earhart:

KHAQQ [the Electra's call letters] to *Itasca*. We are on the line 157 337. We will repeat this message. We will repeat this on 6210 kilocycles. Wait.

And Amelia Earhart was never heard from again.

The United States spent sixteen days and 4.9 million tax dollars trying to find Amelia and Fred. In all, the military covered 250,000 square miles of water, an area roughly the size of Texas. The public was involved too. Amateur radio operators as far away as Wyoming claimed to have picked up her distress signals. Some of the operators were children. Some were women whom Amelia had inspired. Sadly, there was no way to prove where these signals originated or if they were even real. Amelia's husband, George, went days without sleep and bankrupted himself chasing every possible lead. Then, on July 18th, after exhausting all possibilities, President Franklin Delano Roosevelt issued an executive order: All search for Earhart terminated.

Two years later, on January 5, 1939, Amelia Earhart Putnam was legally declared dead.

So, what happened?

No one knows for certain, but communication trouble plagued this flight. Amelia's plane lacked a trailing wire antenna. Some footage suggests the wire snapped upon take-off. Other sources think Amelia had it removed back in the States. This could have been because Amelia wasn't skilled in Morse code, which the wire was useful for. A shame, as the Coast Guard used Morse code to communicate position. In addition, Amelia was operating her radio on one frequency during the day (6210 kHz) and another at night

(3105 kHz), while the *Itasca* was transmitting on 3105 kHz and in Morse code (500 kHz). (The ship didn't have voice capability on 6210 kHz.) It was a perfect storm. Retired Rear Admiral Richard Black worked the radio shack on the *Itasca* during the final moments of Earhart's flight and said the following:

> My firm opinion is that the Electra [Earhart's plane] went into the sea about 10 a.m. July 2, 1937, at a point not far from Howland. If it made a wheels-up landing, it would float, as the gas tanks were empty and the sea was not rough.[*]

According to Chris Williamson of the *Chasing Earhart* podcast, most theories of Amelia's disappearance can be divided into five camps:

1. She ran out of fuel and/or crashed into the ocean. This is the most probable and least exciting of the conclusions. Muriel Earhart Morrissey, Amelia's sister, believed this outcome was true.

2. She was captured by the Japanese as a spy. She either died in captivity or was executed.

---

[*] Daniel F. Gilmore "Did Amelia Earhart Run Out of Gas?" United Press International, June 18, 1982.

3. She became a castaway. In 1940, British settlers found a partial human skeleton on Nikumaroro (formerly Gardner) Island, along with a woman's shoe, cosmetic jars, and an empty sextant (navigation) box. Recent researchers speculate these bones belonged to Earhart, but unfortunately, the bones themselves were lost long ago. In 2019, female skeletal remains found in museum storage on Tarawa Atoll in the Pacific were sent for DNA testing. So far, the findings have been inconclusive.

4. She was captured by the Japanese but survived and returned to live in the United States under an assumed name.

5. She turned around and crashed into an island called Buka. However, based on the location of the last confirmed radio transmission, it isn't plausible that she had enough fuel to travel that distance.

Today, fans, history buffs, and private investors continue the search. They dissect and fine-tune the theories of Amelia's disappearance and launch expensive new expeditions with the latest and greatest technology. A recent example is ocean explorer Robert Ballard, discoverer of the Titanic. His crew dropped two ROVs (remotely operated vehicles) with cameras into the ocean to explore the depths around Nikumaroro. They flew drones overhead. Still, no plane. A small part of me hopes she will be found in my lifetime. But another, larger part loves the lingering mystery. Either way, Amelia's legacy persists as a reminder for us to seek our own adventures.

I'd encourage anyone with an interest in Amelia Earhart, the Ninety-Nines, and aviation to visit Atchison, Kansas, and experience firsthand the place Amelia called home.

> The more one does and sees and feels, the more one is able to do, and the more genuine may be one's appreciation of fundamental things like home, and love and understanding companionship.
>
> —Amelia Earhart, as quoted in *Soaring Wings: A Biography of Amelia Earhart* (1939) by George Palmer Putnam, p. 83

Links:

visitatchison.com

ninety-nines.org

museumofwomenpilots.org

collections.lib.purdue.edu/aearhart/

chasingearhart.com

Selected sources:

"Amelia Earhart Is Down In Pacific: Overshoots Tiny Island On Daring Pacific Hop." *Valley Morning Star* [Harlingen, TX], July 3, 1937, pg. 1.

Butler, Susan. *East to the Dawn: The Life of Amelia Earhart.* Philadelphia: Da Capo Press, 1997.

Fleming, Candace. *Amelia Lost: The Life and Disappearance of Amelia Earhart.* New York: Schwartz & Wade Books, 2011.

Gilmore, Daniel F. "Did Amelia Earhart Run Out of Gas?" United Press International, June 18, 1982, https://www.upi.com/Archives/1982/06/18/Did-Amelia-Earhart-run-out-of-gas/9315393220800/.

Morrissey, Muriel Earhart. *Courage Is the Price: The Biography of Amelia Earhart.* Wichita, KS: McCormick-Armstrong, 1963.

Putnam, George Palmer. *Soaring Wings: A Biography of Amelia Earhart.* New York: Harcourt, Brace and Company, 1939.

Shea, Rachel Hartigan. "Why This Island Is at the Center of a Search for Amelia Earhart." *National Geographic*, June 30, 2017, https://news.nationalgeographic.com/2017/06/amelia-earhart-search-island-dogs/.

Tighar.org—To view the *Itasca*'s call logs and more.

Acknowledgments

From the first few lines, Millie's story had some truly amazing (and patient) champions. A hearty thank-you to my agent, Caryn Wiseman, for being so enthusiastic, wise, and timely with your inspiring news articles of female flyers. You handle my Mayday emails with grace and poise. To my intrepid editor, Sylvie Frank: Thank you for brainstorming numerous plot points and zany ideas. You kept this story on course. I can hardly believe we've reached our destination. Thanks to everyone at Paula Wiseman Books for making this journey so pleasant. Cheers to Sarah Jane Abbott, Lizzy Bromley, Clare McGlade, Randie Lipkin, and Paula Wiseman. Special thanks to Celia Krampien for creating the cover of my childhood dreams.

I'm especially indebted to the Ninety-Nines, Inc. and the Amelia Earhart Birthplace Museum. Louise Foudray, you are a treasure and a font of information. Thank you to Purdue University's Archives and Special Collections for digitizing so much material. I'm grateful to the many journalists, writers, and photographers who carefully documented aviation history.

Thanks to my community of writers: Karen Akins, Leah Henderson, Sally Pla, and Ali Standish. Whether you read bits and parts, a document or texts, you cheered me on. I'm grateful.

Endless gratitude to my friends and extended family for their love and support. I'm the luckiest.

And to my family, my favorite and greatest adventure. We made it. Let's get ice cream.